And that's when her eyes landed on another couple. They were totally oblivious to Dominic's display. No one else in the club was paying any attention to them, but Hannah felt her stomach turn inside out.

Micky.

There was only one door, but they were dancing right near it. No *way* was she going to give Micky the satisfaction of seeing her here alone.

Hannah swallowed. Straightening herself out, she walked onto the dance floor — and headed right for Dominic.

She took a deep breath, then looked deeply into Dominic's eyes. She felt a strange, numbing pain in the center of her chest.

"Please," she said. "Dance with me."

SING

A novelization by A.L. Singer
Based on the motion picture screenplay
written by Dean Pitchford

SCHOLASTIC INC.
New York Toronto London Auckland Sydney

ISBN 0-590-42151-4

12 11 10 9 8 7 6 5 4 3 2 1   9/8 0 1 2 3 4/9

Printed in the U.S.A.   01

First Scholastic printing, February 1989

SING

Chapter 1

Some Christmas, Hannah said to herself. First work, then more work — and then, just for good measure, some *more* work. Other kids were home *eating* turkey with their family, not *serving* it! It seemed that ever since Hannah's father died she and her mother practically lived at the Moonglow Diner.

She quickly ran her fingers through her hair, then stood back and gave the mirror a hard look. Not too bad, she thought. Luckily business was slow today — the less time spent in the kitchen, the less dirty her hair got.

Straightening her dress one last time, she turned toward the door and yanked her waitress uniform off the hook. As always, the same old EMPLOYEES MUST WASH HANDS BEFORE LEAVING sign stared her in the face.

"I *did* already!" she said, flinging open the bathroom door. She knew she had only a few seconds to get outside if she wanted to avoid —

"*Hannahhhhh!*"

Too late. She hated it when her mother screamed her name like that. It was bad enough just *having* a name like Hannah Gottschalk, let alone hearing it ring through the diner like some kind of battle cry!

"Hannah! We're going to be late over at the Tuccis'!"

Hannah rushed through the diner and threw her uniform on a table, right next to a bouquet of flowers still wrapped in paper. For a moment she wondered where the flowers had come from, but she didn't have time to think about that — not with her mother fuming outside. She grabbed her coat and headed for the front door.

On the sidewalk, Rosie Gottschalk fussed over her son Nathan as if he were fourteen months old instead of fourteen years. "Hold that straight, dear," she said impatiently, lifting up one side of the foil-wrapped pan he was holding. "Where's your sister?"

"I'm coming!" Hannah called out as she burst through the front door. "I was working all day, you know — for a slave driver!"

"Well, excuse me! If your father were alive, we could both sit home and watch *Wheel of Fortune*. Let's go, let's go!"

Hannah heard a soft chuckle behind her. She would recognize Murray Bloom's laugh anywhere. She turned to see his friendly, wrinkled face beneath the old winter hat he always wore. Immediately she realized where those flowers were from. Murray had probably given them to her mom — and she'd left them in the diner!

She's really taking him for granted, Hannah thought. Murray was one of the kindest men Hannah had ever met, and he adored her mom. Secretly Hannah wished the two of them would get married. It would make them both so much happier. So what if he was older — as far as Hannah was concerned, her mom should be grateful someone like him cared so much for her.

Now Murray was smiling at Nathan, who sneered and stared blankly ahead. Nathan treated Murray even worse than Rosie did. He acted as if Murray were trying to erase the memory of his father. Sometimes Hannah wondered why Murray even bothered hanging around them.

"Did you have a good day?" Murray asked Rosie as they all started walking up the street.

Rosie rolled her eyes. "Oh, please! We never do any business when school's out. I depend on the kids."

Murray shrugged. "It could be worse," he said. "I stopped by and said good-bye to the Shapiros, you know. They finally had to close up the shop."

Rosie shook her head sadly. "They had a good business. . . ."

Hannah thought she'd wilt if she had to put up with another of her mother's gloomy moods. She turned anxiously to Nathan. "Did Micky call?" she asked. "If you forgot to tell me I'll kill you."

"No," Nathan answered flatly.

"Are you sure?"

Nathan exhaled. "Yes, Hannah," he said, as if he'd told her a hundred times.

"Just *asking!*"

Hannah fell silent. Something wasn't right between Micky and her these days. For two years they'd been so close, so happy together. So why hadn't he called her? She *knew* he was going to Mrs. Tucci's party. No one in this neighborhood ever missed it — no one in all of Brooklyn missed it, it seemed. (If you weren't at the party, it was taken for granted that you'd gotten into a fight with the Tuccis.)

She sighed. Of all the times for Micky to be like this — on a night when she was really counting on him. Her stomach felt like a clenched fist. She had a feeling this night wasn't going to be easy.

Whack! Dominic Zametti let loose a sharp, violent kick. With split-second timing, he jerked his shoulder up, then slashed his arm forward.

Suddenly he felt as if a time bomb had gone off inside him. Every limb, every muscle exploded into lightning-fast, jagged dance moves. *Step, step — kick! Shoulder up, arm out — snap! Hit, hit, pull it together. Cool. . . .*

Then, as abruptly as he'd begun, Dominic stopped. With long strides, he glided silently through the empty bus depot.

A tiny flicker of a smile crossed his face. He had to bust out like that once in a while. Otherwise he'd just explode.

As he pushed open the door that led to the

playground, the hollow *tap-tap-tap* of a basketball grew louder. He stepped outside to see a loose ball bouncing toward him. Over by the hoop, ten of the neighborhood's toughest, slickest players eyed him. Without breaking stride, he grabbed the ball and raced toward the net, weaving his way through the players as if they were traffic cones. Then, at just the right moment, he leaped off the ground, hooked the ball high over his head — and brought it down into a vicious slam dunk.

The ball slapped down onto the blacktop, and Dominic walked coolly away. A barely noticeable nod was the only acknowledgment he gave to the others on the court — but he was completely aware of the reaction he caused over by the fence. Over where Denise Popolato, Margie Green, and Letitia Walker were. Dominic could sense their admiring smiles, and he knew exactly how much to give them — he had it down to an art. Just the slightest, most distracted glance, with only a glimmer of recognition.

Sure enough, that did the trick. He could tell by the way the girls angled their bodies toward him a little more, and chewed their gum a little faster.

The ball came toward Dominic again. Again he grabbed it and charged to the net.

But this time it slipped out of his hands and went careening off toward the 'sidewalk. There was a giggle from one of the girls. Dominic chased after the ball — but it wasn't until the last minute that he saw the four people directly in his path.

He pulled back just in time, barely avoiding a collision with a tired-looking woman. Jerking away from him, the woman cried out in shock. Next to her, an old man reached out to grab her.

Hysterical old broad, Dominic thought. Then his eyes ran up and down the girl next to her. He recognized her from his class at school. Mama's girl. The teachers really love this one. A frightened-looking kid stood near the girl, holding a pan and trying desperately to look cool. Out of the corner of his eye, Dominic noticed that the old man had the ball, and he was glowering angrily. What's this guy's problem? Dominic thought. I didn't kill him or nothing.

He stepped back, looked the guy straight in the eye, and snapped his fingers for the ball.

That made the old man even madder. "Don't you owe this woman an apology?" he demanded.

Dominic turned back around and called out to the players, "Any of you guys got an apology I can borrow? This guy here needs an apology."

There was a split second of tense silence. No one knew exactly what to say. And then it happened — that *feeling*. That strange, electric *thing* that came over Dominic sometimes. It only happened when he knew everyone was staring at him. He could never begin to describe it — but when it happened, he had to do something about it. Something crazy and unexpected.

Whirling around, he grabbed the hat off the old man's head. The woman gasped. Dominic turned to the girl with a wink, put the hat on his own head, and did a quick dance step. "Oh, listen, keep the ball," he said. "I got me a new hat!"

The old man stepped toward him, but the woman held him back. "Don't make any trouble, Murray," she said.

Dominic's face lit up. That feeling was getting even stronger. "Murray?" he repeated, wide-eyed. *"Murray?"*

With an angry snap of the wrist, Murray bounced the ball to Dominic. Dominic caught it and flashed a toothy grin. Slowly, deliberately, he walked up to Murray until the two of them stood nose to nose. Dominic could practically feel the heat of everyone's glare. It made his blood rush. He took the hat off his head and put it back on Murray's. For what seemed like ages, the two of them stared at each other, until Dominic caught a glimpse of a cigar sticking out of Murray's pocket. Inspiration struck again. He pulled it out, stuck it in his mouth, and waddled away in a hunched-over duck walk. "Hey, Murray!" he said, flicking the cigar like Groucho Marx. "Murray Christmas, huh?"

Murray's face turned red. With a defiant gesture, he took the woman's arm and began walking away.

As Dominic watched them, he heard the woman muttering, "I wish I had a gun. I swear to God, Murray, sometimes I wish I had a gun."

He smiled and began to turn away — but not before he caught the look on the girl's face. A look so full of hate that if it *were* a gun, he'd be history.

Chapter 2

"Murray — Rosie! Merry Christmas! Happy Chanukah!"

Mrs. Tucci's voice rang out over the deafening noise of the party. Murray and Rosie smiled and hugged her, as if nothing had happened on the way. Nathan ran inside, looking for a place to put his pan down. But all Hannah could think about was "Murray Christmas," and it made her boil inside. At least she wasn't feeling sorry for herself anymore — or worrying about Micky.

She walked into the house and squeezed her way through the crowd toward the den. As usual, all the adults were in the living room, stuffing their faces and talking about leaky roofs, snowblowers, mortgage rates, and whatever else adults talked about. And, as usual, there were heaping platters of food on a table by the wall — it looked like enough to feed a small country, but Hannah knew it would be gone within hours. She glanced around at the same Christmas and Chanukah decorations she'd seen for the last who-knows-how-many years. Mrs. Tucci never threw anything out.

Finally she reached the den, where the *real* party was. All her friends hung out in there every year — that was the good part. The bad part was that Cecelia Tucci had been taking piano lessons, and the den was where the Tuccis kept the piano. It was just Hannah's luck to be walking in at the moment Cecelia sat down to play.

Standing by Cecelia, with a look of adoring rapture on his face, was her boyfriend Aristotle Thermopoulos. No one knew Ari very well. It was hard to find anything in common with him because he had only one interest — Cecelia. And his interest went way beyond her looks (which weren't bad) and her personality ("pushy" was the mildest word to describe it). No, Ari loved Cecelia for her talent (that's where he was *way* off), and he was determined to bludgeon the world into sharing his feeling.

Hannah began to have a sinking sensation. She'd started to think of Micky again. He should have been in there, but he was nowhere to be seen. I hope nothing happened to him, she thought. Just then she spotted her friend Tiffany Schwartz, who gave a smile and a little wave.

"Have you seen Micky?" Hannah asked her.

Tiffany shook her head and shrugged.

Hannah surveyed the room again. Over by the piano, a few girls had gathered around to sing along with Cecelia. Suddenly Cecelia made a face and stopped playing. When everyone fell silent, she raised an eyebrow and said, "This song really sounds better with just one voice."

Ari's beefy face burst into a proud smile. Fiddling excitedly with the gold chain around his neck, he shushed everyone.

The last thing Hannah saw before she left the room was the look of utter disgust on almost every face.

Maybe Micky was in the kitchen. Hannah made her way there, just as her best friend Naomi was coming out.

"Hannah!" Naomi cried out happily. Then a sudden, concerned expression shot across her face. She stood in the kitchen doorway. "Uh, I don't think you want to go in there — "

"How do I look?" Hannah asked.

"Nice . . . good! Yeah." Naomi's eyes darted back toward the kitchen. "But I still don't think you want to — "

Without answering, Hannah barged past her. Naomi never acted this way unless something was up.

Hannah had read Naomi exactly right — and immediately she wished she hadn't. On the plus side, she'd finally found Micky. But on the minus side, she found someone else with him — and that someone else happened to be very pretty.

And very intimate.

"Hi, Micky," Hannah said coldly.

A look of embarrassment flashed across Micky's face. The girl quickly backed away from him. With a small gesture that seemed to say "See you later," she slipped out of the kitchen.

Micky smiled nervously and gave Hannah a tense kiss.

"Long time no see." Hannah's teeth were gritted so tightly she could barely get the words out.

Micky let out a deep breath. "Yeah. . . . Listen, Hannah, I need to talk to you."

With that, he took her arm and led her through the house to the back porch.

Hannah started shivering as soon as they stepped outside. She wasn't sure if it was the cold or her fear about what Micky was going to say.

His breath formed little white puffs in the frigid air as he looked down at his shoes. "Hannah, whatever we had was beautiful. The last two years have been . . . *you* know. They really have."

You can do better than that, Hannah wanted to say. She could feel tears welling up just behind her eyelids.

Micky shifted his weight from foot to foot. ". . . but I'm finding I'm a man with a lot of interests and a great thirst for life — a thirst you don't seem to share, I might add. I just can't be held down at this time."

Held down? Hannah felt as if her insides had been ripped out. Micky's words pounded in her head like sledgehammers. She could hear voices shrieking at her to *do* something — argue with him, yell at him, hit him!

But maybe there was hope. Maybe he was just going through a phase. If she lashed out, she'd *really* lose him. Hannah felt completely paralyzed. This can't be happening to me, she thought. Not now. Not on Christmas.

"Rosie! Come over here!" Mrs. Tucci called out. "Did you meet Theresa Lombardo? She's Vinnie's cousin. She just moved back here from Cleveland, and she's teaching over at the high school next semester."

Theresa Lombardo smiled, gearing herself up to meet yet another parent. She had a warm feeling being back in Brooklyn, but there was something a little suffocating about this party. Maybe it was the circle of smiling mothers standing around her, who didn't seem to want to move until they had her whole life story. She was dying to go into the other room, where there was the sound of a piano — and younger voices.

"Well," said Rosie with a wan smile, "at least we got one more semester. That school's been threatening to fall down for years. But lookit — eighty-one years, and it's still there." She shrugged and looked over toward the other room. "Oh, listen, the kids are getting ready for Sing. You know about Sing?"

Miss Lombardo's face lit up. Of all her memories of Brooklyn, "Sing" was the one thing she never got tired of talking about. In her neighborhood, just about every kid would dream about being old enough to appear in it. You could be smart or stupid, athletic or wimpy — but once you got to high school, you were equal with the rest of your class when you went on that stage.

And if your class's musical was judged to be the best, you never forgot it the rest of your life. Sing had been a tradition for forty years, surviving Big Band, be-bop, jazz, and disco. And Miss Lombardo was happy to know that it was holding strong right on through heavy metal and hip-hop.

"Rosie," Mrs. Tucci said before Miss Lombardo could open her mouth, "Theresa was born in Brooklyn."

"Born in Brooklyn?" Rosie said incredulously.

Miss Lombardo nodded. "Bay Ridge."

"*Bay Ridge?* I don't believe it! Here I am yapping away — Bay Ridge, huh? And you still got your natural hair color."

Miss Lombardo let that comment fly. Within seconds, Rosie and Mrs. Tucci were heading over toward the other room — and Miss Lombardo was left facing all the other mothers. She felt a little like a swimmer who'd wandered into a circle of sharks.

"So you're back at your family's since the divorce?" one of them asked.

"Umm, no," Miss Lombardo replied. "My mother died last year. I live alone."

"You got children, I hope!" another woman said.

Miss Lombardo knew it was useless to get out of a situation like this. In this kind of neighborhood, everybody found out everything before long. "We didn't have any children," she said matter-of-factly.

The women backed away from her in stunned

silence. And then came the question. She was waiting for it; she knew *someone* would ask it. Still, the words cut through her like a knife.

"How *old* are you, dearie?"

Years ago Miss Lombardo wouldn't have minded that question at all. But nowadays it was loaded with meaning. What these women were saying to her was: A woman already into her thirties with no husband or children is a woman without a life.

Smiling as politely as she could, she said, "Excuse me," and walked toward the den.

They were wrong. They were all wrong, Miss Lombardo thought. It *was* possible to have meaning in your life without kids and a mortgage and an attached two-family house. She wasn't exactly sure how she would find that meaning in Brooklyn, but she knew she'd do it somehow.

Pulling herself together, Hannah raised her head. She tried to look Micky in the eye, but he turned away. "Couldn't we just wait? Just a week — until after New Year's? Couldn't we wait until then? It doesn't have to mean anything. . . ."

Micky squirmed and looked around like a caged animal. Hannah clung to the slightest change in his expression.

But before he could answer, the screen door flew open. "There you are, the two of you!" came Rosie's voice. "Get in here! The kids are going to sing!"

"Later, okay?" Hannah snapped.

14

But Rosie seemed oblivious to Hannah's tone of voice. She threw an arm around Micky and gave him a hug. "Micky, bring her in here! It's the school song! You know it's traditional."

Obediently, Micky held the back door open. Hannah shot him a look and then brushed past him into the house. Rosie pulled both of them toward the den, where the strains of the Brooklyn Central High School song rang out.

Hannah felt completely humiliated. Naomi was giving her pitying looks. How many other people knew about Micky? Hannah wanted to run out of the room, but Micky beat her to it. She saw him slip out as soon as Rosie loosened her grip.

Now everybody was singing, but Hannah could barely hear the words. It all sounded like some big, shapeless echo rattling around inside the empty shell that used to be Hannah Gottschalk. She was vaguely aware of Cecelia starting to sing at the top of her lungs, acting out the words to the song. She was barely conscious of Mr. and Mrs. Tucci beaming with pride, and Naomi rolling her eyes, and Ari elbowing Naomi in the ribs.

Not long ago, Hannah might have found it all funny. She would have joined the singing and felt warm inside. But now none of it mattered. It was all a silly, meaningless spectacle.

All of a sudden Hannah caught sight of her brother Nathan, who looked miserable. Old Murray had just put his arm around him. Poor kid, Hannah thought. He'll never get over Dad. She looked around to see everyone hand in hand, swaying to the music — for a moment parents and children were equal, kids who hardly ever *spoke* to their mothers and fathers were holding their hands. . . .

And that's when the floodgates burst, the tears that Hannah had been holding back for so long.

As she sobbed quietly, she felt a warm pair of arms around her. It was her mother, rocking back and forth, singing proudly. She had no idea what was going on in Hannah's head.

But at this point, Hannah had to take what she could get. She leaned her head on her mother's shoulder and rocked sadly to the beat of the song.

Chapter 3

"Taxi!"

Miss Lombardo watched the cab glide by her. It figures, she said to herself. They're off-duty whenever the weather turns bad.

She bundled herself up against the freezing wind and walked toward the bus stop.

"Yo! You want a cab?"

Miss Lombardo turned around with a start. Behind her was a man wearing a thick muffler and a ski mask. She smiled with relief. "Oh! Yes, please."

The man walked into the street, looked left and right, and put his fingers to his mouth. He let out a sharp, shrieking whistle. A speeding Checker cab suddenly screeched to a stop, skidding right by them.

When the cab backed up, the man held open the back door.

"Thank you," Miss Lombardo said, stepping into the cab. "Thank you very, very much — "

Before she could close the door, she felt a sudden yank on her shoulder. She gasped. A hand had closed around the strap of her purse. Instinctively she pulled back — and the purse fell to the street, spilling everything inside it.

The man in the ski mask grappled for it, but Miss Lombardo thrashed at him, swinging her arms wildly. Pushing open the front door, the cab driver jumped out and began to run around to her side.

But the masked man was strong — and quick. Miss Lombardo didn't stand a chance of out-muscling him.

Just as he was about to pull the purse loose, she made one last desperate try. She lunged for the man's hand with her teeth, and clamped down hard.

"YEEEEEEOOWWW!" The man screamed and ripped his hand free. Then, without a single backward glance, he ran off into the night.

Shaking, Miss Lombardo picked up her purse and stuffed the contents back in.

"You okay?" the cab driver asked, standing over her.

"Yeah . . . fine . . . fine. . . ."

The driver looked after the mugger, then shook his head. "Boy, you're lucky," he said. "I didn't punch the meter yet."

Rosie Gottschalk had been right. Brooklyn Central High School was like some old crumbling fortress that had withstood generations of battle. Miss Lombardo surveyed the lobby in quiet awe. Students were crammed over by the entrance, where uniformed security guards scrutinized them from head to toe. It was hard for her to get used to that — it was a far cry from her school in Cleveland.

She could sense students' eyes burning into her, as if sizing her up for the kill. Smiling, she adjusted the collar a little higher on her neck, trying to cover up the bruise she'd gotten in her mugging. Then she walked through the lobby toward her homeroom.

When she passed the school's trophy case, she stopped briefly to peer inside. Decades worth of banners, photos, and plaques were jammed together — all celebrating Sing. Faded, fresh-faced kids with ducktail haircuts, glowering hippie types with peace necklaces, blown-dry Barry Manilow clones in white suits. . . . Where were they all now? Miss Lombardo wondered. Probably selling insurance, building houses, worrying about their own kids. But if they wanted, they could always come back here to look inside and recapture a little immortality.

"Brings back memories, Miss Lombardo?" came a voice from behind her.

She spun around to see the school principal, Mr. Marowitz. He smiled warmly and gestured toward the case.

"What? Oh . . . oh, yes!" She laughed. "What's Brooklyn without Sing?"

"Good," Mr. Marowitz said. "I'm glad you said that." He took her by the elbow and led her through the crowded halls. "We haven't spoken about this yet, but you know, we're woefully understaffed again this semester — " Just then his attention was caught by an older woman across the hallway. "Lydia!"

A cigarette dangling from her mouth, the woman walked over to join them.

"Lydia Simonides," Mr. Marowitz said. "Theresa Lombardo. Theresa is going to be with us this semester. In fact, she's our new senior-class Sing adviser!"

Miss Lombardo felt stunned. "Really?" She looked at Mr. Marowitz in disbelief. "Whoa! I mean . . . um . . . I'm honored!"

"You'll get over it," Mrs. Simonides said flatly.

"No, you don't understand," Miss Lombardo replied. "I mean, the chance to work with these kids, to make a difference in their lives — "

Mrs. Simonides raised her eyebrow. "Ach, a missionary! Sunshine, can I make a suggestion?" She reached out and touched Miss Lombardo's hoop earrings. "Students here tend to catch their fingers on these."

Miss Lombardo gulped and touched her ears protectively. She watched as Mrs. Simonides walked away. Against a nearby wall, she spotted a boy standing spread-eagled as a security guard frisked him.

"Excuse me," Mr. Marowitz said to Miss Lombardo. He walked over toward the security guard. "Whatcha got, Hector?"

The guard handed him a top-of-the-line Rolex watch.

Mr. Marowitz examined the watch, then went

up to the boy. "And where'd you get this, Mr. Zametti?"

The boy looked over his shoulder. His dark eyes glared at Mr. Marowitz. "My brother gave it to me for Christmas. Got a problem with that?"

"Where'd your brother get it?" Mr. Marowitz pressed.

The boy looked at him defiantly. "He saved up box tops."

Mr. Marowitz toyed with the watch, then gave it back to the guard. With a flick of his head, he indicated that the guard give it back. "Now, Mr. Zametti, you only have to learn how to tell time."

The boy lowered his arms from the wall and turned around. He was lean and tough-looking; one of his hands was bandaged and the other wore a weight-lifting glove. And when his glance met Miss Lombardo's, she felt a chill run through her.

Mr. Marowitz took her arm again and steered her down the hall. For some reason, the boy's look was stuck in her mind. There was something about him. . . .

Moments later a black woman passed by them, dragging a student by the neck. "This one — hello, Phil — this one, he says he ate all his homework because the devil made him do it." She pushed the boy toward the office marked Principal.

Mr. Marowitz was about to answer, but he was distracted by the sight of two men in business suits waiting outside his office. "Terrific, Felicia," he muttered, "I've got the Board of Education nosing around again. Oh, uh . . . Felicia Devere, meet Theresa Lombardo. Excuse me."

Miss Lombardo was now alone with Mrs. Devere. She smiled meekly.

Mrs. Devere immediately caught sight of the neck bruise and shook her head. "Darlin', darlin', darlin'," she said. "We gotta get you some running shoes."

With that, she threw back her head and cackled at her own joke. As she walked away, Miss Lombardo nervously fingered her earrings. What kind of school was this, anyway?

Chapter 4

Dominic Zametti. Miss Lombardo read the name to herself off the seating chart. She wasn't going to have any trouble remembering *his* face. She glanced down the list, trying to memorize which student belonged to which name: *Hannah Gottschalk, Naomi Leitner, Micky Glaser.* . . .

Holding a stack of announcements, she stood up and looked out over the class. Right away she knew it wasn't even worth trying to smile. Nothing was going to penetrate the dull, lifeless eyes that stared back at her.

She paced up the aisles and started to read: " 'Over the Christmas vacation, a crack developed in the swimming pool, and all the water has leaked out. So anyone who had hoped to try out for the swim team is urged to consider an alternate sport.' "

"Ohhhhhhh," came a groan from some of the students.

The groan startled Miss Lombardo — it was sarcastic, not real. But the ones who did it were at least paying attention, she realized. Everyone else was just chatting away, completely ignoring her.

Ahead of her, a long pair of legs was draped across the aisle, blocking her path — Dominic's legs. She stopped reading and looked at him. "Excuse me, can I get you to put both feet on the floor?"

Silence. Not even the slightest acknowledgment.

"Uh . . . excuse me?" she repeated.

"I don't do tricks."

That wasn't the answer Miss Lombardo had expected. And when the snickering began to build around her, she began to see red.

But she wasn't going to let him win this one. Calmly she began reading again: " 'This afternoon your last period will be canceled — ' "

A chorus of cheers burst out.

Whack. Without missing a beat, Miss Lombardo yanked the chair out from underneath Dominic's feet. They crashed to the ground, but Dominic pretended not to notice.

So did Miss Lombardo. " 'You are required to be at the elections for your Sing leaders for the spring semester — ' "

Another groan. Out of the corner of her eye, she saw one girl pass a note to another. Hannah . . . Naomi, she thought, placing their names with their faces.

" ' . . . this is the forty-first year for Sing at Brooklyn Central, and because of decreasing enrollment, this year, for the first time, the sophomores and juniors will combine their efforts to compete with the much more experienced seniors.' " She stopped reading and looked up. There had to be *some* way to get these kids' attention. "Is that true? Are you seniors really more experienced?"

The strategy worked. Practically everyone responded in some way — giggling, laughing, passing rude comments. Now, Miss Lombardo thought, if I can get them psyched about Sing. . . .

All of a sudden Dominic spoke up. He was grinning and looking at an unfolded piece of paper in his hand. "You want to hear experience? You gotta hear this: 'Naomi. . . .' "

Hannah whirled around, looking panic-stricken.

" ' . . . Micky's been avoiding me all morning,' " Dominic went on, reading as if he were a third-grader. " 'You gotta talk to him. He's breaking my heart —' "

Before he could finish, Hannah flew across the room in a rage. "You monster! You monster!" she shrieked, clawing at Dominic.

Miss Lombardo rushed over to pry them apart. Around her, students howled with laughter. " 'He's breaking my heart! Breaking my heart!' " Dominic shouted melodramatically.

He pulled away, but Miss Lombardo grabbed the note from him. To her surprise, Dominic grabbed it right back. She stood paralyzed, not knowing what to do next.

Brrrriiinng! Just then the bell rang, ending

homeroom. As the students bolted out of their seats, Hannah reached around Dominic and snatched the note from his hands. Red-faced, she ran out of the room.

Dominic met Miss Lombardo's glare. With a smirk, he held out his empty hands and strolled out of the classroom, laughing.

In seconds Miss Lombardo found herself alone in the room. She felt her knees weaken. Slowly, she sat down at one of the desks.

This is supposed to be a school, she said to herself. Looking around, she saw all the signs: blackboard, chalk, an eraser, chairs. . . .

But somehow it all seemed like a mirage. She could have sworn she had stumbled into a war zone.

Mrs. Devere put her hands on her hips. Her piercing eyes looked out over the underclassmen who were sitting in the gymnasium. Behind her, Mr. Marowitz looked on admiringly. "And after you've elected your Sing leaders today," she said, her voice strong and clear, "after you've written your show, after all the auditions, and rehearsals, and the sweat and tears, will you stand there finally, onstage, drunk with the intoxicating thrill of victory? Or will you cower before the hideous spectre of humiliating defeat?"

Nathan felt a rush of excitement. He *knew* the underclassmen would win the show. Sure, he could tell the juniors were a little apathetic. But Mrs. Devere was going to be such an inspiring adviser — and besides, *his* class, the sophomores, had all the enthusiasm and all the best talent.

He gazed across the room at Zena Ward. When it came to talent, she could outshine anyone in the school, Nathan thought. Not to mention the way she looked. He drank in every move of her lean, perfect body, the way her brown skin seemed to glow from a special light within. When she glanced in his general direction, he waved. As usual, she didn't respond. Maybe next time, Nathan thought. At least she doesn't hate me.

" . . . and remember," Mrs. Devere went on, "you're going to be in this together. It's not the *sophomores'* songs, or the *juniors'* costumes. You may not know each other, you may not even *trust* each other — "

Nathan heard Cecelia Tucci say, "I hate the sophomores."

"*I* hate the sophomores," her boyfriend Ari replied.

"Oh, Ari," Cecelia squealed, "we hate the same things!"

Oh, gag me, Nathan thought. It was going to be hard to actually *like* the juniors, if they were all like those two!

Suddenly an expectant hush came over the gym. Mr. Marowitz was handing Mrs. Devere two envelopes. Nathan crossed his fingers. He knew exactly who *should* be elected Sing leader.

"Okay, from the sophomore class . . ." Mrs. Devere ripped open one of the envelopes. "Zena Ward!"

"*All riiiight!*" Nathan hollered. The other students burst into applause. Like a TV game-show host, Mrs. Devere yelled, "Come on down!"

Zena, smiling with disbelief, ran to the front of the gym.

"And Zena's co-leader is a *junior*!" As one of the students gave a drumroll on the side of the bleachers, Mrs. Devere squinted at the paper in her hands. "I gotta pronounce this? Aristotle . . . Ther . . . mopoulos!"

Ari leaped up into the air and shouted triumphantly. He turned to Cecelia and locked her in a long kiss.

Mrs. Devere raised an eyebrow. "Honey," she said to Ari, "some things should be done in *private*!"

Miss Lombardo heard the cheering of the sophomore class all the way to the auditorium. She couldn't believe their enthusiasm — in here, it felt like a ward for the terminally bored. She looked down and started counting the votes for senior class leader.

"Uh, Miss Lombardo?" a voice whispered above her. "Hi . . . I'm Micky Glaser. . . ."

She looked up to see a handsome boy with a pained look on his face, as if he had some secret he needed to tell her. She glanced down at her list. A huge number of votes was next to Micky's name.

"It's looking good," she said to him with a smile.

Micky nodded solemnly. "Yeah, that's what I'm afraid of. This year I have a problem . . .

well, lots of problems. My family . . . my father's sick . . . well, it's really my mother . . . and, see, my grandmother's recently started coughing and coughing — ”

“Yo!”

Startled, they both turned around. Next to them, holding out a ballot in his bandaged hand, was Dominic.

“Can I leave?” Dominic said. “I voted.”

Miss Lombardo froze. Theresa, how could you be so blind? she said to herself. The right hand is bandaged . . . the same hand that —

A voice floated back into her memory: “Yo, you want a cab?” There was no doubt whose voice it was — Dominic's!

She felt herself starting to shudder. Calm down, she said to herself, meeting Dominic's glare. “What did you do to your arm?” she asked.

“Hangnail. Look, can I — ?”

“Zametti, right?”

Dominic looked surprised, but only for a split second. “Yeah . . .” he said cautiously.

“Anyway, Miss Lombardo?” Micky interrupted.

Rage welled up inside Miss Lombardo. Rage mixed with fear. She held up her hand, signaling Micky to wait. There was something she had to settle with Dominic Zametti.

“Look, uh, I got plans, okay?” Dominic said.

Out of the corner of her eye, she spotted a security guard leaving the room. If she called him now. . . .

But no. There was a better way to deal with

this. "No . . . no. Sit down, Mr. Zametti. I still think you might find this interesting."

Dominic and Micky both skulked back to their seats. Quickly, Miss Lombardo tallied up the votes. "Okay," she announced, facing a sea of completely indifferent faces, "one of your leaders is . . . Hannah Gottschalk!"

The applause was so weak she could barely hear it. Hannah, instead of looking excited, seemed tense.

"And Hannah's co-leader . . . now this was a close one . . . I'm sure you've all got your own personal favorites. . . ." She noticed Micky squirming, looking as uncomfortable as Hannah did. " . . . but I've counted and recounted and there's no doubt about it. Your leader for Sing victory this year is . . ."

Dominic let out a yawn.

" . . . DOMINIC ZAMETTI!"

Cool as he was, even Dominic couldn't keep his eyes from bugging out.

Chapter 5

"Micky wasn't elected? And you were? Hannah, you can't organize that thing by yourself!"

Can't she leave me alone? Hannah thought. She walked away from her mother, trying to put on her waitress uniform at the same time. It was bad enough having been elected Sing leader — all she needed now was another job. *Micky* was the one who liked to do that kind of stuff. The only reason Hannah even thought of getting involved was to be with him. And now. . . .

"Look, honey," Rosie said softly. "I'm only thinking of you. That's so much work for you! And you don't seem very happy about it."

Hannah sighed impatiently. This really wasn't any of her business, and besides, there were customers outside. . . .

"Yes, yes, I notice everything," her mother continued. "And yet you should be having the time of your life! Look at me — I'm a dishwasher up to my elbows six days a week. Where's *my* enjoyment anymore?"

Hannah threw her arms in the air. "Murray's crazy for you, Mom." She walked around Rosie and pushed through the kitchen doors.

"Oh . . . *Murray*," Rosie said, following close behind. "Look, when you're fifty, it's different. It's not like Micky — "

Hannah whirled around. "Momma! I am no longer seeing Micky! It's over!"

Rosie gasped.

Suddenly Cecelia Tucci's familiar whiny voice called out from one of the booths, "Hannah, could we get some water over here?"

"How long you been coming here?" Rosie snapped. "Get it yourself!" Then she turned to Hannah. "What 'over'? How could you walk away from — ?"

"*He* walked away from *me*!"

"And you let him go? You couldn't hold on to him? What kind of a woman does that?"

"*Aaaaaaghhhh!*" Hannah's scream pierced the air. Every face in the diner turned to look at her.

In the stunned silence, Hannah picked up her pad and walked to Cecelia's table. Then, calmly, as if nothing had happened, she asked, "May I take your order?"

The pizza was pretty good today. A little greasy, but pretty good. Dominic stared at the posters behind the counter. He was bored with Margie Green and figured if he ignored her a little she'd get the message.

He was right — before long, she walked away. Dominic grabbed for some extra garlic salt.

"Mr. Zametti?"

Dominic stopped chewing. What idiot in her right mind — in *this* neighborhood — would call him Mr. Zametti? He turned around — and almost spit out his pizza.

Miss Lombardo was standing behind him, holding out a sheet of paper. "I brought you a tentative rehearsal schedule."

"What?"

"Well, you left so quickly — "

Dominic swallowed his pizza. "Look, Miss . . . what's your name?"

"Lombardo. *Miss* Lombardo."

"Yeah. See, I don't want to be in show business — "

"Who does? Nobody does this 'cause they want a career. We do it for the experience and for the fun."

Dominic smirked. "Hey, I got other ideas about fun."

"I'll bet," Miss Lombardo said dryly. She pulled out a manila file from a pile of books she was holding. "I was very surprised, Mr. Zametti, to dig out your school files and discover a record of petty larceny and assault — "

"So, I got a temper," Dominic replied.

" — and that you're on court-ordered probation?"

"Yeah?"

"See, I've been out of Brooklyn for a while, but I thought that, while on probation, there were certain things you didn't want to do. . . ."

"Like what?"

Miss Lombardo shrugged. "Oh, like mugging a woman who's climbing into a taxi on a cold Christmas night — just to make up a wild situation. . . ."

Dominic couldn't believe his ears. "What? — I never did anything like that!"

"See, I wouldn't have thought so, either. You don't strike me as that stupid." She pointed to his right hand. "But if we were to have that bandage removed, and if, as I suspect, there are teeth marks underneath — *my* teeth marks — you could spend the next semester and a few more years bunked out in a cell on Riker's Island. You might even find yourself sharpening a toothbrush handle to use for self-defense in the yard — hoping the guards don't turn their backs and leave you at the mercy of some slobbering, four-hundred-pound murderer."

"Heyyy — "

"So you see, Mr. Zametti, you can spend the next three-to-five eating slop from an aluminum tray in a filthy prison cafeteria — *or* you could show up and serve your class as Sing Leader." She gave him a sweet, calm smile. "Either way, I've got you!"

Dominic gave her a big, sexy grin. You're just

talking big, aren't you? he thought. You wouldn't. . . .

Miss Lombardo's smile widened. But it had lost its sweetness. In fact, there was something about it that made Dominic's blood run cold. Something that said she meant business.

Chapter 6

Hannah scooped out a hunk of leftover strawberry cake with her hand. The Moonglow Diner had closed up long ago and she didn't care how much of a mess she and Naomi made. She stuffed the cake into her mouth and licked the frosting off her fingers. A tear fell from her cheek. It landed on the frosting and gave it a salty taste. "I'm going to miss him . . . so much."

"Look, Hannah," Naomi said, wiping her lips, "Micky was a kick. But come *on* — he had *hair* all over his back!"

Hannah's eyes widened. She exploded with giggles.

"He does!" Naomi insisted. "He does! I saw!"

They both screamed out laughing and slid to the floor. The cake landed between them with a dull *splat*. That made them shriek even more. Hannah clutched her side. The whole situation was so . . . so. . . .

Terrible! Suddenly Hannah's eyes filled with tears. In an instant her laughter turned into sobbing. "Micky's gone and I get stuck doing Sing with a sleaze. What am I going to do, Naomi?"

Naomi stopped laughing. Her face became solemn as she considered Hannah's question. Finally she looked up at her friend, pointed at the smashed cake on the floor, and announced her solution:

"Eat."

Zena Ward sang softly, practicing with a couple of backup singers. She was only one of the many sounds in the gym. Dancers' feet slapped the wooden floor in rhythm, singers warmed up — every corner echoed with sophomores and juniors practicing for their auditions.

But to Nathan, there wasn't another person in the whole room but Zena. Every move of her lips, every nuance of her voice transfixed him. Behind her, the two singers smiled broadly, swaying to her song.

And that's when Nathan noticed Ari bursting into the room, followed by Cecelia and a group of her friends. Nathan was sure Cecelia would melt with jealousy as soon as she heard Zena sing. But instead, she just gazed smugly around the room and adjusted her spangled Rockette costume. Her jaw worked over a piece of gum, sending little snapping noises into the air. Beside her, Ari gestured emphatically to Blade Vallone. Blade was in charge of the scriptwriting for the show — but judging from the miserable look on his face, he wished he'd never taken the job.

"Look," Ari insisted, his voice booming out

over the sounds of the rehearsal. "I'm not saying that a Romeo and Juliet story is a *bad* idea. It's a start. But where, pray tell, is Cecelia in all this? I am looking here at these scenes and I do not see any part that calls for Juliet to tap-dance — "

"She doesn't twirl a baton once!" Cecelia complained.

"And splits — Cecelia does great splits!" Ari crowed proudly. "Show him your splits, honey."

Cecelia took the gum out of her mouth and stuck it under her arm. Immediately she collapsed to the floor into a perfect split.

By this time, Zena's voice was wailing out above the din. Nathan wanted to listen, but Ari began shouting even louder. "What I'm looking for here is a vehicle for Cecelia, you know what I'm saying?"

Blade couldn't take it anymore. He wheeled around to face Ari. "You want a vehicle? Put her under a bus."

With that, he walked away.

Ari sputtered with anger. "Hey! What are you — ?" He spun around to see his friends staring at Zena and moving to the beat of her song.

"Ari, I'm not happy," Cecelia said.

Ari's face was red. He waved his arms, trying to get everyone's attention. "People . . . hey, I'm trying to . . . what's going on — ?"

It was hopeless. But instead of shutting up, Ari marched over to Zena — and slapped his hand over her mouth. "Some of us are trying to work here!" he bellowed.

Zena's eyes popped open in shock. She pulled away from him, rigid with anger. But Ari rolled right on. "I am in the middle of a scriptwriting committee meeting right now. Have you got anything to add to *that* discussion?"

"Yeah," Zena replied viciously. "Add this." She turned her back to him, signaled Blade to start playing the piano, and began singing at the top of her lungs.

Nathan smiled. She sounded great even when she was angry. Blade, pounding on the keys, threw his head back in laughter.

But Ari wasn't amused. He stalked over to the piano and slammed the top down on Blade's hands.

"Yeeeeeoooow!" Blade screamed.

"Oh, get over it!" Ari retorted. Indicating Cecelia with a passionate sweep of his hand, he said, "You're not the only one in pain here!"

As Cecelia hung her head with a pout, Nathan had the urge to burst out laughing. He had always suspected it, but now he knew for *sure* that Ari and Cecelia were visitors from *The Twilight Zone*.

Thwap.
Thwap.

Hannah looked at her watch. This was worse than waiting on tables. She *knew* she'd be a terrible leader. The faces of the so-called "senior scriptwriting committee" stared blankly into the air.

Thwap.

Thwap.

And if Dominic didn't stop throwing his rubber ball against the auditorium stage, she was going to scream.

"Well," Miss Lombardo finally said, "you've got synthesizers; Clarissa's offered to write the music; and if Wilson's father can get hold of those strobe lights, then what kind of a show would you use them in?"

For the first time during the whole meeting, Stanley Wlodkowski spoke up. Stanley was an All-City tackle on the football team. Non-jocks said he could only do twenty reps at each weight machine because that was as far as he could count. "A disco?" he suggested excitedly. "How 'bout you got these guys in a disco? And they dance!"

The others groaned.

A really stupid idea, Hannah thought, but at least a start. Maybe this would get everyone talking. "And then?" she asked.

Stanley shrugged. "I don't know. Then they sing, I guess."

Silence settled over the auditorium like a heavy cloud.

"I'll write it down," Naomi said dully.

Then, from the first row of seats, Dominic snickered.

Stanley shot out of his seat. "What's so funny?" he shouted. "You got something to throw in here? Huh?"

"Whoa, whoa, whoa," Dominic said.

"Well, do you?" Hannah asked. "Do you have anything to add?"

Dominic smirked. "Hey! Hey!! I'm the leader here. I don't gotta have ideas."

"Well, then shut up!" Stanley snarled.

At that, Dominic sprang out of his seat and lunged for Stanley. Screams rang out as several of the girls ran out of the auditorium. "Get the guard!" one of them yelled.

And as Hannah looked on in horror, the two boys began pummeling each other. Her meeting had disintegrated before it had even started.

Chapter 7

Instantly six guys jumped on top of Dominic and
Stanley. All Hannah could see was a mass of
flailing fists. She stood frozen as the sounds of
grunting and scuffling echoed through the big
hall.

Within seconds the group tore the two boys
apart. Two muffled *whomps* resounded as Dominic and Stanley were thrown into seats.

And that's when the security guard came running down the aisle.

Miss Lombardo wasted no time taking control.
"Oh, thank you for coming," she said calmly. "We
were just having some creative differences. I'll
handle it."

"I'm going to have to file a report," the guard
replied, eyeing Dominic suspiciously. "This
guy — "

"*I'll* handle it!" Miss Lombardo suddenly
shouted.

The guard looked at Miss Lombardo quizzi-
cally. With a shrug, he turned to leave.

His retreating footsteps were the only sound in the auditorium as everyone nervously settled back in.

Hannah could practically see the steam come out of Miss Lombardo's ears. Quickly she cleared her throat and broke the tense silence. "So . . . we are no closer to a show than we were. Any more ideas?"

"Look," Dominic said, his voice laced with anger, "you can take your lasers and put 'em on an island in the middle of the ocean and sink 'em for all I care!"

That set off a flurry of responses. "Lot of help you are," someone called out. Around him, everyone murmured in agreement.

"Wait, wait!" a voice shouted out. Hannah looked back. It was Wilson, whose father was going to supply the show's lighting. "An island that sinks! Think about it — like the lost continent of Atlantis!"

The other students stopped talking.

"I could write some water music," Clarissa volunteered.

"Yeah . . . with all these high-tech sets and stuff . . ." another boy added.

Soon the whole auditorium began to buzz about the idea. Dominic looked around, first to Miss Lombardo and then to Hannah.

He flashed a self-satisfied grin. "Can I go now?"

They were only cassette tapes, but they were just sitting out there on the sidewalk. Sitting among the piles of merchandise outside a discount store, just asking to be taken.

Without looking down, Dominic scooped one of them into his pocket and kept on walking.

HONNNK! He jumped at the sound of a car horn.

"Look at that strut! What style! What grace!"

Dominic's face lit up when he heard his older brother's voice. "Freddy!" he called out.

Freddy Zametti brought his new Cadillac to a stop right beside his younger brother. He leaned across the front seat as Dominic squatted to look inside. "What are you doing — besides terrorizing the neighborhood?"

Dominic shrugged. "You know. . . ."

"How's school?"

"I'm flunking everything, as usual."

"Well, listen, Einstein. You ready for something a little more profitable?" Freddy grinned knowingly.

"You bet!"

"You busy tonight?"

"Yeah, I could — " Suddenly Dominic stopped himself. "Oh, wait a minute, man . . . I got this stupid thing at school . . . aw, Freddy, there's this teacher, she's doing a number on me. How about next time?"

Freddy shrugged. "Don't say I didn't ask you. Maybe next time."

Before his brother could reach for the gear shift, Dominic said, "Hey, Freddy?"

It didn't take much, just a certain placement of the eyebrows, and Dominic knew Freddy would understand what he wanted.

Freddy smiled. He reached into his pocket and handed Dominic a wad of money. Then he pulled a fistful of watches out of a cardboard box on the car seat and shoved them into Dominic's hands.

"Whoa, Freddy!" Dominic said, amazed.

"It's been a good week, all right? Come here, give your brother a kiss."

Dominic obediently bent down to the window. Freddy kissed him on the cheek. "How's Mama and Poppa?" he asked casually.

"They're still saying rosaries for you."

Freddy let out a small laugh. "Tell 'em to keep praying."

As Freddy pulled away, Dominic stuffed the watches and the money into his pocket. He gazed in admiration after his brother. The minute I leave the old man's house, that's exactly the way I'm going to be, he vowed to himself. Free to do what I want, answering to nobody! He felt a sudden burning sensation when he thought of where he had to go that night.

Especially to no lousy teacher.

Chapter 8

"Underclass rules!" a group of juniors and sophomores shouted into a video camera. Around them a loud cheer went up.

Nathan had goosebumps. He hadn't expected the auditions to be like *this*. The hallway outside the gym was jammed. Off to his left someone practiced scales on a xylophone as a tuba player blasted away nearby. A unicyclist rode up and down, past a group of dancers and a kid with a bow and arrow. Singers were warming up, actors were going over lines — and off in a corner a girl was yodeling.

I have to compete against this? Nathan thought. He wished he were a couple of years older. According to his sister, the senior auditions were nothing like this.

Just then the door to the gym opened and Ari stuck his head out. "Keep it down out here!" he yelled.

Immediately the hallway settled down.

"And remember," Ari went on, "I am only looking for *true* talent."

He quickly shut the door behind him — to a barrage of nasty comments. Right away everyone began to practice again — and Nathan continued to wonder why on Earth he'd bothered to show up.

Stanley's face was as expressionless as a rock during his audition. He stood with his feet planted as if the offensive line were about to attack him. And his voice was so monotonous, Hannah could barely tell he was singing.

Dominic looked at her in stunned disbelief. Before he could say anything stupid, she politely waved to Stanley and said, "Uh, thank you. That's all we need to hear for now."

Clarissa stopped playing the piano accompaniment, and Stanley lumbered off the stage. Hannah crossed her fingers as the next girl came on. The past week had been a horrible nightmare — could it possibly be that not one person in the class had any talent? Was this going to be some sort of Sing all-time record — the first tone-deaf, flat-footed senior class in history?

And to make matters worse, Dominic had been at every audition. Hannah couldn't figure out why he even bothered showing up. All he ever did was brood and shout "Next!" in the middle of people's performances.

"Like a virgin . . . hey! Touched for the very first time. . . ."

Hannah gripped her pencil stub tightly. She

didn't know how much more of this she could take. Not only did the girl sound like a moose, but she was so big she made Stanley look dainty.

"WHOA! STOP THE MUSIC!"

Hannah jumped at the sound of Dominic's sudden, anguished shout. The girl on stage looked crushed.

"Do you *mind*?" Hannah hissed.

Dominic jumped out of his seat. "Yes, I *mind*!" He ran to the stage and leaped onto it. The girl backed away, her eyes wide with confusion.

"Do you mean to tell me," he shouted back to Hannah, "that *this* is the best you can do?" He gestured to the girl, then said to her, "No offense, sweetheart."

Mortified, the girl stormed off the stage.

Hannah was furious. "I don't see you moving your big Italian rear end to help out!"

"Honey, you don't *know* what this Italian is capable of!"

"Well, I for one am dying to see!"

Just then Miss Lombardo interrupted. "No, I'd say we *all* are." She looked up at Dominic, who was now standing center stage. "What did you bring us to sing, Mr. Zametti?"

With a mischievous smile, Clarissa began playing some all-purpose chords on the piano.

Dominic's face turned white. "Oh, now wait a minute. . . ."

Hannah just folded her arms. She was going to enjoy watching him squirm.

But Dominic pulled himself together and walked toward her, a look of defiance on his face.

"All right, all right," he said. "You want talent, I'll get you talent." He whirled around to Clarissa. "Yo, let's have some rock-and-roll! A one, a two, A ONE, TWO, THREE, FOUR!"

Clarissa's hands flew over the keys, although no one knew exactly why. Instead of performing, Dominic just strode out of the auditorium.

Hannah and Miss Lombardo exchanged a baffled look. Clarissa just shrugged. "I need the practice anyway."

She continued playing, and Hannah went backstage to apologize to the auditioners. There were still a few left — the ones that hadn't been scared away by Dominic. Hannah collected their music and lined them up.

All of a sudden Hannah heard a loud thumping on the stage. She spun around. There, flinging his leather jacket into the pit, was a student she barely recognized — one of the greasers who always hung around shop class.

"I don't believe this," one of the auditioners muttered.

And neither did Hannah. In fact, her mouth fell open. At first she thought he was up there to mock the audition. But he wasn't.

He was there to dance.

Hannah hadn't seen anything like it. With explosive moves, his body gyrated to the beat of Clarissa's song — jumping, slashing, kicking in perfect rhythm.

Where — ? How — ? Hannah shot a glance out to Miss Lombardo, who was sitting in the audience, flabbergasted. But out of the corner of her eye, she caught a familiar figure in back of the auditorium.

A cocky half smile flickered on Dominic's face before he turned to the exit and walked back out.

The next few days passed like a whirlwind. Each day there were four or five new students at the audition. Students Hannah had never met — or wanted to meet. All friends of Dominic.

Who would have thought that Denise Popolato could sing? Hannah thought she only moved her mouth to chew gum. Not to mention Margie Green and her friends — Hannah always knew they could shake their hips when guys were around, but who knew they could actually *dance*?

By the beginning of the next week, there were just enough good people to put on a show. By Wednesday, Dominic had begun choreographing.

And by Friday, Hannah and Miss Lombardo found themselves staring at a killer dance number featuring Margie, Denise, and three more of the toughest girls in the class. This is outrageous, Hannah said to herself. They can sing, too!

Everyone bounced to the music, as the words resounded to the back of the enormous room. It was electric. The girls spun into a finale that sent up a huge roar from the other seniors, who all sprang to their feet.

Hannah sat bewildered. It wasn't exactly her idea of a cast, but it would have to do.

He must have bribed them, she thought. With who knows what. . . .

Reluctantly she joined in the applause — and then her eyes met Dominic's. A broad, arrogant grin stretched across his face. "You gotta trust me," he said. "Just trust me."

Hannah threw Miss Lombardo a look. Smiling like a person who'd just been sprung from prison, Miss Lombardo shrugged. Well, he did it, she seemed to be saying.

Hannah folded her arms. He *did* do it, but that didn't mean she had to like him. Some things would always be impossible.

Chapter 9

Hannah gasped. "Oh, they're gorgeous!"

She pulled a string of pearls out of a jewelry box. Across the table, her grandmother gave her a crinkly smile and said, "You're only eighteen once!"

Rosie gave Hannah a stern, proper look — the kind of look she only gave on rare occasions like this, when the family was actually *eating* in a restaurant instead of working in one. "What do you say, Hannah?"

"I was getting to that!" Hannah answered. She stood up and wrapped her arms around her grandparents. "Thank you, Grandma, Grandpa!"

Kissing the two of them, Hannah felt warmer and more relaxed than she'd felt in weeks.

But that feeling lasted only another few seconds. At the front door, the maitre d' was struggling to keep someone out.

"I got a friend over there. 'Scuse me!"

The voice was unmistakable — Dominic's. He

was with a slick-looking guy and a girl, both older than he.

Hannah sank into her chair to hide — but it was no use. She cringed in horror as she heard him yell across the room, "Yo, Hannah!"

"Hello, Dominic," she answered tightly.

"You believe this place? They want me to put on some crummy jacket. I told them to forget it." He caught sight of the gift wrapping on the table. "Somebody having a birthday?"

"It's Hannah's eighteenth," Hannah's grandmother said. "March eleventh!"

Dominic's face broke into a wide smile. "No kidding! You know, me and Hannah're running this Sing thing over at the school."

Hannah's grandfather raised an eyebrow. "Is that so?"

"Yeah," Dominic answered. "Kind of like I get the ideas and then she agrees with me — huh, Hannah?" He reached over the table and grabbed a breadstick. "You don't mind?"

Hannah wanted to *die*. It was bad enough she'd had to work with him all winter and spring — did he *have* to show up to spoil her birthday?

If I ignore him, he'll just go away, Hannah chanted to herself. It didn't help that her mother was making wild head movements as if to say, "Get him out of here."

"So," Dominic continued, his mouth full of breadsticks. "You must be Hannah's mother." He extended his hand to Hannah's grandmother.

Hannah thought Rosie was going to blow a fuse.

The old woman beamed. "Her *grand*mother," she said.

Then Dominic turned to Rosie. "Don't tell me, don't tell me . . . her sister?"

Rosie's furious expression melted on the spot. She smiled modestly. "No, I'm the proud mother."

"And it's Murray, ain't it? Murray? Murray Christmas?"

A shot of recognition flashed across Rosie's and Murray's faces. Over two months had passed since they'd seen Dominic on that basketball court, and they'd forgotten him — almost. Rosie's smile disappeared.

Dominic shook Murray's hand energetically. "It's great to see you again! Lookin' good! Lookin' good!" Then he gestured to another table, where his two partners were sitting. "Okay, gotta go. May I say it has been a sincere pleasure to meet all of you. And Hannah. . . ."

Hannah reluctantly looked up.

"Happy birthday, huh?" he said.

For a split second she forgot how much she hated him. His smile actually had some *warmth* in it, his eyes a little sparkle.

But she wasn't going to let that slimeball think he could charm her. She scowled at him, just before he turned to walk away.

A gloomy silence settled over the table. Hannah's grandparents looked bewildered, and Nathan was trying to keep from cracking up.

With a hollow, disgusted look on her face, Rosie pushed aside her plate. "I can't eat."

She had taken the words right out of Hannah's mouth.

Dominic couldn't believe his eyes when he walked into the auditorium the next night. He watched in agony as Hannah tried to lead the girl dancers through a routine. What is this, an aerobics class for geriatrics? he thought. He knew Letitia and Margie could dance, but even they couldn't make this pathetic combination look good.

He had to do something about it. "Miss Lombardo!" he shouted. "I cannot perform my duties if Hannah here keeps interfering. I bring her ripe talent — "

Hannah whipped around. "And then *I* have to teach them how to dance!"

"That?" Dominic shot back angrily. "That's not dancing! That's organized pain! You wanna see real dancing — "

"Yeah, I wanna see *real* dancing!"

" — you gotta go to the clubs — go to the Heat Wave or the Silver Hammer!"

Hannah sneered at him. "Oh, yeah? Who died and made you the dance maven?"

Miss Lombardo immediately stepped in. "That's an excellent idea, Dominic. When could you — ?"

Who asked for her two cents? "What?" Dominic said, wheeling around.

"You and Hannah. If you hate the choreography, then you ought to do some research."

"I ain't going nowhere with her! Besides, you two got a lot of stuff to do. It is now the middle of March, doll, in case you haven't noticed. You only got six weeks."

"Mr. Zametti. Let me make myself perfectly clear. Where the interests of this show are concerned, I will stop at nothing to do the best Sing possible." Miss Lombardo narrowed her eyes angrily. "Nothing. *Capisce?*"

You little. . . . Dominic wanted to put her in her place, make her realize who she was fooling with. But he felt powerless, paralyzed by an image that was stuck in his head. An image of his parole officer's angry face, examining the bite mark on his right hand.

Dominic gave Miss Lombardo a cold, hard look. You really think you can wrap me around your finger, huh? he thought. Well, it ain't gonna be as easy as you think. . . .

Hannah spent the evening trying to decide exactly what people wore to a place like the Heat Wave. She tried on about five combinations before settling on one.

But as she and Dominic walked through the parking lot to the club, her stomach sank. She'd gotten it all wrong. There were three different styles there — cheap, glitzy, and both of the above. If polyester were gold, the Heat Wave would be Fort Knox.

She followed Dominic into the club, through a

sea of pompadours and sequined dresses. One of the girls spotted Dominic, and when he got close, she kissed him on the ear.

Hannah knew the type — man-killer dress, makeup slathered over every inch of the face. *Made* for a guy like Dominic.

Dominic ignored her and pushed his way through the entrance. Hannah tried to take his arm, but he shook it aside. He stopped by an empty table near the dance floor and pointed to one of the seats. "You can see from there," he said matter-of-factly. "You want something to drink, there's sodas at the bar. You wanna dance, there's the floor. You wanna leave, there's the door."

Hannah felt helpless. I don't believe it, she thought. He's just going to leave me here. "Why are you being like this?"

"This?" Dominic echoed. "This wasn't my idea."

On the dance floor, the girl who had kissed Dominic swept by them, dancing with another guy. Without even acknowledging him, Dominic stepped in front of the girl and began to dance.

The guy must have known Dominic — instead of protesting he just skulked away, deflated.

Hannah sat down and looked around nervously. Over by the wall was a group of guys who didn't have dates — and with good reason. She shrank into her seat. What if one of these creeps actually asked her to dance?

I'm here to do research, she kept telling herself. She turned her eyes toward the dance floor — and found herself staring at the writhing body of Dominic's partner.

Hannah pulled back to avoid being smacked in the face. But she could tell that the girl had nowhere else to dance, because of the way Dominic had positioned himself.

He's doing this on purpose, Hannah realized. Just then Dominic whirled around provocatively, putting himself right in front of her. She pulled back again, fuming. Spare me, Dominic. I'm really dropping dead with desire for you.

As the music got louder and faster, Dominic spun the girl out into the center of the floor. Her long legs flashed into the pulsating light, as Dominic's body sliced through the crowd.

Almost instantly the center of the floor cleared out. Hannah blinked. Was that really *Dominic*?

Hot wasn't the word to describe the way he danced. Each sharp thrust, each jagged shoulder movement was like a shot of electricity. She sat in awe, suddenly forgetting how awkward she felt.

And that's when her eyes landed on another couple. They were totally oblivious to Dominic's display. Their bodies were wrapped around each other in a close embrace, swaying to the music. No one else in the club was paying them much notice, but Hannah felt her stomach turning inside out. She remembered the girl — Hannah had met her at Mrs. Tucci's Christmas party. The same guy was with her then, too.

Micky.

Hannah bolted up from her chair. She was torn between the urge to run, the urge to scream, and the urge to throw up. She looked around desperately for a way out.

There was only one door, but Micky was dancing right near it. No *way* was she going to give him the satisfaction of seeing her here alone.

Suddenly Hannah felt like the loneliest girl in Brooklyn. Her mother's words came back to her: *"You let him go? You couldn't hold on to him? What kind of woman does that?"*

She couldn't listen to that old-fashioned, twisted logic. She couldn't get down on herself for something she had no control over. Micky was a jerk. He didn't deserve her, and someday she'd make him realize it.

Like right now.

Hannah swallowed. Straightening herself out, she walked onto the dance floor — and headed straight for Dominic.

The music had changed, and so had the lighting. A soft ballad was playing now, full of longing and vulnerability. The club was dark, except for a few washes of blue light. Dominic's back was to her; his arms were wrapped around the girl as they stood by the side of the dance floor. Slowly Hannah approached. For a few seconds, she stood behind him, feeling her heart beat.

And then she tapped him on the shoulder. Gently.

He turned around hesitantly, as if he weren't

sure if the touch was intentional. When he saw it was Hannah, he had to look twice.

Hannah took a deep breath, then looked deeply into Dominic's eyes. She felt a strange, numbing pain in the center of her chest.

"Please," she said. "Dance with me."

Chapter 10

Dominic's eyes probed hers. Half of her hoped he'd say no. Maybe there was another way to get back at Micky — a way that wouldn't involve dancing with the biggest troublemaker in Brooklyn Central High.

Dominic looked back at the girl, then at Hannah. He furrowed his brow and turned his back to both of them.

Slowly, silently, he walked onto the dance floor.

Hannah swallowed. She'd expected him to at least *say* something. Ignoring her was the cruelest thing he could do.

But when he got a few steps away, he turned around. He stared from Hannah to the other girl. With a tough, almost begrudging look, he gave a small nod.

To Hannah.

She gulped. Her eyes quickly darted toward Micky — she wanted to make sure he was in her line of sight. He was, but obviously it was going to take a lot to get his attention away from his sexy, *cheap* new girlfriend.

And Hannah was determined to do just that. She walked toward Dominic with her arms raised, inviting him to hold her closely.

But he was already dancing — alone, lost in his own world.

You self-centered little. . . . This wasn't going to be easy. She grabbed his hands, forcing him to dance.

Dominic backed away, glaring at her. He cocked his head and held up his hands, then beckoned her toward him. *He* was going to be the one to lead.

That was fine with Hannah — almost. Dominic's dance moves were cool, distant. And they were getting nearer and nearer to Micky.

Quickly Hannah pulled Dominic closer and wrapped her arms around him. For a moment, he froze. Then a smile crept across his face. Hannah looked away.

His right hand traveled in a circle around her back, then descended slowly . . . down her spine . . . below her waist. . . .

Easy, pal. She gave him a sharp look and pulled his hand back up.

They swayed to the music. Hannah never let Micky out of her sight. But after a while, something else was distracting her.

Dominic.

He wasn't trying anything sleazy, he was just

dancing. And he was wonderful. Hannah had never moved like this before. With Micky, she'd always just assumed that her feet were two targets — they always got smashed a few times during the slow dances. But with Dominic, it was different. He made her feel as if she were floating across the floor on a cushion of air.

She smiled. Closing her eyes, it was easy to pretend he was someone else. Someone whose personality matched the way he moved — graceful, sensitive. How could someone who danced like this be so tough and angry?

Her eyes blinked open and she gazed up into his face. He certainly wasn't bad-looking. It seemed silly, but if she didn't know who he was, she could almost *like* him.

Then Hannah felt a cold rush. Micky had turned and was looking straight at her.

She gave him a smug, nonchalant nod. A nod that said, Oh, yes, I vaguely remember you. She pulled Dominic even closer, and he held her tighter.

Micky stopped dancing. He said something to his girlfriend, and the two of them walked toward the exit.

It had worked, even better than Hannah had thought it would. She pulled away from Dominic. He'd served his purpose.

As she watched Micky leave, she wanted so badly to feel triumphant. But there was nothing inside, no feeling at all. She straightened out her hair and her dress.

Dominic followed her glance, then looked back at her. When he spoke, his voice was soft. "I don't know why you're knockin' yourself out over him. . . ."

His words cut right through to her heart. With a polite smile, she said, "Thank you for the dance," and walked back to her seat.

Nathan elbowed his way through the crowd outside the gym. In front of him there was a stream of excited yelps and frustrated moans as students read the casting list on the door.

Off to the side, an unmistakable voice cut through all the rest. "I *know* you put in a solo for me, Ari. But how come I'm not playing Juliet?"

"They're blind, Cecelia. They're idiots and they're blind."

"I don't wanna be in a losing show!"

"Honey, I *swear* we'll win this year." Ari lowered his voice. "I got ways. Believe me, I got ways."

Blowhard, Nathan thought. By now he'd finally made his way to the front. He scanned the list. There was Zena's name, and Cecelia's. . . . Suddenly his eyes stopped. There it was, next to the words *SPEAR CARRIER* at the bottom of the page, in bold, black letters:

NATHAN GOTCHALK

He let out a whoop and threw his fist in the air. Who cared if they spelled it wrong. He was going to be in Sing!

* * *

Miss Lombardo shifted uncomfortably and looked around the jam-packed teachers' lounge. Actually, "lounge" seemed like a ridiculous name for this place — "holding pen" was more like it. There couldn't be a worse place to have a meeting of the entire teaching staff. She hoped Mr. Marowitz would say whatever he needed to say and get it over with.

But when he stepped to the front, she couldn't help but feel a shiver. For some reason he looked older. She hoped nothing awful had happened to him.

When he finally spoke, his voice was subdued. "Brooklyn Central has been an institution in this neighborhood for over eighty years. But now, after putting off the decision, the Board of Education has decided that at the end of this school semester — "

He broke off and took a deep breath. "At the end of this school semester, Central will close its doors and cease to operate as an educational institution of the city of New York."

Miss Lombardo felt herself gasp. Other teachers cried out with shock. Was this some sort of joke?

Mr. Marowitz wasn't smiling. If anything, his expression had become even more glum. "I'll leave it up to each of you to handle this news with your students as you see fit. Classes will end on schedule. Athletic teams won't be affected . . . but I'm afraid that there will be no final Sing at Central this year."

That was it. End of speech. The worst for last.

Miss Lombardo couldn't believe her ears. Her new job — her new *life* — had been yanked away from her. To her left, crusty old Mrs. Simonides was actually starting to cry.

Mr. Marowitz stood there for a few seconds. A murmur of voices began — first helpless, then angry and defiant. He cast a glance over to Miss Lombardo.

But she couldn't face him. Right now, she couldn't face anybody. As gracefully as she could under the circumstances, she lowered her head into her hands and began to cry.

Chapter 11

Hannah ran toward the Moonglow Diner. She hoped her feet would leave the ground, or the diner would transform into a huge green monster. Then she'd know she was only having a nightmare, and the news about Brooklyn Central High was part of it.

No such luck. Her feet ached from the running, and the diner looked as solid and drab as it always did.

She pushed open the front door and stopped short. Rosie stood in the center of the dining room, surrounded by neighborhood mothers clustered in the booths and tables. It looked as if they were in the middle of a meeting.

"This is going to hurt us all," Mrs. Tucci was saying. "But *you*, Rosie. . . ."

Rosie waved Hannah into the kitchen and followed her. Behind them, Mrs. Tucci called out, "We're not going to take this lying down! We're going to fight it!"

The other mothers mumbled their approval as the kitchen door swung shut.

Hannah stood facing her mother in the empty kitchen. On a nearby rack, the pots and pans hung like battered stalactites. It felt funny *standing still* in there — no orders to place or pick up, no cooks and waiters slamming around.

For a long time now, Hannah hadn't shared much with her mother. Neither of them seemed to have much time, especially after her dad died. Rosie had had the diner to worry about, and Hannah had her own life — all those evenings rushing away after work to be with Micky, and then Sing.

But now all of it was going up in smoke. Hannah felt that with one stupid Board of Education pronouncement, her entire life had been wiped out.

She looked into her mother's eyes, and what she saw made her heart sink. For the first time, Rosie looked like an old lady. There was a hollowness Hannah had never seen before.

"Momma?" she said, almost involuntarily.

For a moment, Rosie's bottom lip quivered. Then, as if finally releasing a lifetime of grief, she burst into tears. "What's going to happen to us? They're not just closing down the school . . . they're closing down the neighborhood! Where are we going to go? I *live* for these kids!"

Hannah took a step forward. She remembered her mother comforting her when she was a little girl. Back then, before life got so complicated,

Rosie had always been there for her. Maybe now it was time to return the favor.

Tentatively, Hannah reached out and folded her mother into her arms. Rosie clung to her, burying her face in Hannah's shoulder. The two of them rocked back and forth, slowly, as if making up for lost time. . . .

Whack. Their moment was broken by the sound of the kitchen door slamming open. They turned to see Nathan, looking pale and shattered. Hannah felt her heart opening toward her brother. He looked from her to Rosie, not knowing what to do.

Then, without saying a word, he reared back with his foot and kicked a pile of pots, sending them clattering all over the kitchen. One by one, he attacked them again, his eyes burning with despair.

And neither Hannah nor her mother raised a finger to stop him.

"So what's going on — you're free all of a sudden? You don't got that Sing-along garbage anymore?"

Dominic ignored the question. He clenched and unclenched his fingers around the steering wheel, watching the reflection of the streetlights off the storefronts as he drove by. Yeah, easy for you to make small talk, Freddy, he thought. All you gotta do is sit in the car. Dominic *hated* going along with Freddy on one of these "jobs" — he always got stuck with the dirty work.

And the worst part about it was that he was scared. No matter how hard he tried to hide it, he always felt all cold and tangled-up inside.

"What's the matter with you?" Freddy exploded. "All the time you're complaining about how you want to taste the high life with your brother Freddy — and then the time comes and you're chicken!"

Freddy burst out laughing, but Dominic just stared straight ahead. Somehow it just didn't feel right. He knew he was going to be up all night worrying about this. If anything went wrong, if his parole officer found out about it, the only vehicle he'd be driving for the next few months would be a prison lawn mower.

"Okay, left up there . . . good." Freddy squinted, then pointed to a spot up ahead. "Now cut the lights. And pull up right there."

Dominic followed his brother's finger to a storefront in the middle of the block — and his eyes suddenly popped open.

It was the Moonglow Diner.

"What? Here?" he said, panicked.

"Not here, you jerk! Around the back!"

"But wait! You can't!" Dominic protested.

"What?"

Dominic felt a wave of panic shoot through him. "I know the people who own this place!"

"The old Jewish broad? So?" Freddy was starting to sound angry. As the car slowly pulled into the alley behind the diner, he looked around nervously.

"So? You're not gonna knock this place over, Freddy?"

A flash of light made them both stiffen. Behind them, another car approached. As it glided through the alley, neither Dominic nor Freddy moved a muscle.

Slowly, it disappeared out the other end.

"*Freddy!*" Dominic pleaded.

Thwack! Freddy wheeled around and smacked his brother in the face. His eyes blazed with anger. "What? You got a problem, then get out of here. You're the one moanin' all the time. Go on! Get out!"

Dominic felt his face flush with shame. He'd never let his older brother down like this.

Freddy sat back and pulled himself together. "You don't want to go inside? Fine! You wait in the car — with the motor running. And don't do nothing, understand?"

Flinging open the car door, he jumped out and disappeared around the side of the diner.

Dominic's hands were shaking as he got out and waited by the side of the car. A few weeks ago he wouldn't have cared about this place. Sure, he might have been a little jittery, he would have hated Freddy for making him do it — but really, it was nothing to pop a place like this.

But things had been happening to Dominic, and Freddy hadn't even bothered to notice. Freddy laughed about Sing; he figured Dominic was in it just to pick up chicks.

Well, it wasn't like that. Dominic didn't need

Sing — he could have whatever girl he wanted, anytime. But Sing needed him. And he didn't have to do much — all he had to do was the same kind of stuff he did in the clubs, and everybody went nuts.

Besides, some of those goody-goody types were all right. Like Hannah. She was a good kid. Not someone who deserved to be ripped off in the middle of the night.

So what was he doing here?

"Yo, Dominic!"

Dominic nearly jumped out of his skin. He whirled around to see Blade Vallone passing through the alley with a guitar in his hand. Blade gave him a cheerful wave and kept on walking.

Dominic waved back, trying to keep from looking like his whole life was passing before his eyes.

But when Blade disappeared into the night, Dominic collapsed against the car. It was a good thing Sing night was going to be canceled. The way it looked now, he was going to be spending that night looking through iron bars.

Chapter 12

Hannah ripped open a plastic packet, and the smell of fresh-roasted coffee beans burst into the air. At least they didn't steal these, she thought. She looked around sadly at the diner. At a table in the middle, Murray was trying to comfort Rosie as she talked to her insurance man. It was bad enough that school was closing, which would be terrible for business — but to be *robbed* at a time like this? Hannah sighed and poured water into the top of the coffee maker. At least they would be able to collect the insurance. She wished she could understand what this guy was saying — all this mumbo-jumbo about deductibles was confusing.

Finally the man sat back and put down his papers. He gave Rosie a sympathetic look. "Basically, Mrs. Gottschalk," he said, "the policy that your late husband had for theft has lapsed. Your loss of four thousand dollars *would* have been covered if you had remembered to — "

Rosie cut him off with a feeble noise that was

halfway between a laugh and a cry. "Don't tell me that! Don't tell me what I should have done!"

Hannah almost dropped the coffeepot.

Rosie looked up at the insurance man, her face etched with pain. Her lips quivered as she spoke. "I can't tell you . . . I wasn't meant to live like this. One day I've got a healthy husband, the next day he's as cold as marble. And Harry. . . ."

What is she saying? Hannah felt scared. Her mother never got like this; she never babbled on to total strangers about Dad. "Momma?"

". . . Harry leaves me what? Two kids and a restaurant falling down in a dying neighborhood. How do I prepare myself for something like this? How do I deserve a life like this?"

Murray stroked her back. "Rose . . ." he said gently.

"You don't know!" She practically spat her words out at Murray. "Twenty-one years with one man. You can't even understand what it's like to be left! Harry! How could you? How could you? I hate you, Harry! I hate you!"

She lunged for the table, swiping her arm across it. Silverware and saltshakers flew onto the floor with a crash.

Horrified, Hannah rushed across the room and grabbed hold of her mother's flailing arms. She pulled them toward her and wrapped Rosie in a big hug. Slowly Hannah rocked her back and forth, trying to calm her. "Don't you think we all miss him?" she asked softly.

Rosie pulled away and sank into a nearby

booth, sobbing. "He was *my* Harry. He was going to take care of me."

Hannah stood still, dumbfounded. At the table, Murray hung his head and the insurance man shuffled some papers.

Just then the back door opened. Hannah's eyes darted over to see Nathan rushing toward her. He was pulling Blade Vallone behind him.

"Go ahead. Tell her," Nathan whispered.

Blade looked frightened. "I don't want to get anybody in trouble."

"Tell her!"

Blade took a tentative step toward Hannah, out of sight from Rosie's table. "Well . . . ummm . . . last night. . . ."

Dominic stalked down the school hallway. When he got near the cafeteria, he picked up speed. There was a huge sign on one of the walls. He didn't have to read it, he'd seen the words before:

SAVE OUR SCHOOL!!
BOARD OF EDUCATION HEARING
WEDNESDAY 4:30
PROJECTED ATTENDANCE:

Underneath the headlines were three giant tagboard thermometers that were labeled SOPHOMORES, JUNIORS, and SENIORS. Dominic could see that they were already near the one-hundred-percent level.

As students rushed between classes, Margie,

Denise, Nathan and a few others were trying to recruit people to come.

The whole thing was such a waste of time. Dominic strode toward the front stairs.

But before he got there, he heard pounding footsteps behind him. "Dominic! Slow down!"

He turned to see Miss Lombardo racing toward him. "Are we going to see you at the Board of Ed? We're going to need all the help we can — "

"Why bother?" He continued walking.

"Dominic, wait a minute! They're not just closing the school. They're going to cancel Sing! And that show is practically yours! What happens to everything you did?"

"Sell it to the movies. I don't care."

Miss Lombardo's voice softened. "Hey, look. I got you into this. Just show up, help us out — and I'll forget everything, our little deal."

Right, Dominic thought. Well, it's too late now. Nothing matters now. He turned back toward the stairs —

And felt a sudden body blow from behind! Losing his balance, he tumbled down the stairs.

What was going on? He grabbed onto a bannister for balance and looked up to see his attacker.

Hannah!

Before he could stand up, she grabbed him by the collar and threw him up against the wall. "You slime!" she screamed.

"Hey! Hey!" he protested.

"How could you do that to me?"

"I don't know what you're talking about!"

"That's a lie!" She pulled back her fists to hit him.

Dominic grabbed her arms. "I swear!"

Hannah's eyes burned into his. " 'Trust me,' you said! How could anyone trust you?"

"What? Hannah, *what did I do?*"

"You want me to answer that? You are a *liar* — and you are a *thief!*"

Dominic took a wary step back. He could sense a crowd gathering around them. "You don't know what you're saying!"

"Then how come you're trying to run?"

That was the last straw. *No one* made a fool of Dominic Zametti. "What do you know?" he said through gritted teeth. "You ain't nothing but a piece-of-dirt waitress!"

Hannah looked as if she'd been electrocuted. She hauled off and smacked him across the face.

She caught him by surprise, and it stung. He scanned the circle of people around him and saw Miss Lombardo staring bitterly. He met her glance, looked back at Hannah, and ran out the front door.

Chapter 13

Freddy squinted at his brother through half-asleep eyes. He pulled his bathrobe tight around him and watched Dominic pace around his apartment.

Normally Dominic wouldn't have gotten his brother out of bed, but he had to talk to him tonight. After all, if his brother couldn't understand his feelings, who could?

"Look, Dominic," Freddy said, "you pay your money, you take your chances."

"But if somebody saw me there — I mean, just suppose — and I was to get caught — "

"Look, what do you want? I don't make no guarantees! You're always looking at me, wanting what I got — "

"I never seen Papa getting his like that."

"Papa's scraping!" Freddy replied. "He always has. He's scratching around for a life in a neighborhood that went belly-up years ago. I tried it like Papa — and then I got smart. And soon, I'm getting out. You ought to think about doing the same. Otherwise you're gonna end up like everybody else around here — a nobody!"

"That's not true! Everybody here's got a name!"

"And you know why you're gonna be a nobody? Huh? Because you think big, but you don't got the guts to grab it! Not like me!" He snarled at Dominic. "You think you're so smart!"

Dominic shut his mouth. There was no arguing with Freddy about stuff like this. But still, Freddy was his big brother. . . .

"I feel bad, Freddy," Dominic said softly.

Freddy sneered. "So what."

Hearing that forced Dominic to open his eyes. Freddy *never* made anything better for him. Freddy made things better for *Freddy* — and that was it. Even his girlfriends were like cars that he tired of and changed every year.

Suddenly Dominic's dreams about his own future seemed to fall apart. What was his life going to be about? Destroying families, ripping out the hearts of working people just like his dad — for nice cars and a nice apartment *if* he could keep out of jail?

The eyes, Dominic, he said to himself. Look closely into your brother's eyes. That's *you* in a few years, man. Do you want it?

Slowly, painfully, Dominic started to leave.

Freddy looked at him with a sudden, playful grin. He grabbed Dominic and ruffled his hair. "My little brother . . . I do love him!"

Dominic yanked himself away and ran off, slamming the door behind him.

Hannah was steaming mad. She couldn't believe that *these* men — this bunch of sour-faced, self-important jerks — were going to be the ones to decide the fate of her life.

She especially hated the one who was trying to quiet everyone down. Mr. Frye was his name. Mr. Frye, whose stuffy, sweating face glowered under the worst toupee Hannah had ever seen. All she could think about was that she wanted to make *him* fry.

"I don't know how to make it any clearer to you people," Mr. Frye said, looking exasperated. "Central is a depressed high school."

The crowd exploded. From the seats, the aisles, and the walls of the packed conference room, people shouted back to him, "We ain't any worse than Fenimore!" "What about Verazzano?"

Everyone had something to say, it seemed — Rosie, Murray, Mr. Marowitz, Mrs. Simonides, Mrs. Devere, Miss Lombardo. . . .

Mr. Frye bellowed over the tumult, "This decision has come down from Albany, from the State Board — and there is no changing it. I — we *all* appreciate your feelings here, but in June this school is going to be closed. For good."

The room began settling into a helpless silence.

"These gentlemen . . ." Mr. Frye gestured to the men behind him. ". . . will begin working at the school Monday to oversee the orderly — and final — disassembly of the school plant. Please give them your fullest cooperation. Thank you."

As he quickly gathered up his papers, Hannah and Miss Lombardo both jumped to their feet. Their frantic words overlapped.

"No! Wait a minute!"

"That's it?"

"What about Sing?"

"What are you going to do with our Sing?"

Mr. Frye lifted a sheet of paper and read from it. " 'All extracurricular activities will be terminated.' " He looked back out to the crowd. "We don't have the budget."

A loud grumble went up in the room, and Miss Lombardo shouted over it. "Now wait just one minute! Every year, for forty years, every high-school class in Brooklyn has staged this show! And with every passing year, it's become more and more of a — a — "

Hannah finished her sentence. "It's a part of this community! A tradition!"

"Yeah!" Miss Lombardo replied. "That's what I'm trying to say!"

All around, people began shouting in agreement.

"This is a community in crisis, Mr. Frye," Miss Lombardo continued.

"And that is precisely why *this* is happening!" Mr. Frye shot back. "Do you think *I* personally am doing this? Do you think we *invent* these statistics?"

Mrs. Tucci leaped to her feet. "What do statistics have to do with a school show?" She reached next to her and pulled Cecelia out of her seat. "My daughter here made her own costume!"

Another parent stood up and said, "And my boy! He works hard after school!"

"Mr. Frye! Look at this!" Hannah turned at the sound of Ari's voice. "Show 'em your splits, Cecelia!"

As Cecelia slid obediently to the floor, ignored by everyone, other parents began jumping up and joining the protest. Mr. Frye glanced back to his associates and rolled his eyes in frustration. "I'm sorry," he announced, "this meeting is adjourned."

Hannah was mortified. This couldn't be *it*! She looked helplessly at Miss Lombardo.

And then, from the back of the room, came a loud, violent, "HEY — NO WAY!"

Mr. Frye whipped around in shock.

Hannah looked back to see someone pushing through the crowd to the front of the room — Dominic! For a brief moment, their eyes met. She turned away in anger.

"Security!" Mr. Frye yelled.

A guard grabbed Dominic, but Dominic shook him aside. "Hold it, hold it. Take it easy," he said.

"Young man, you are out of order!" Mr. Frye called out.

Casting a quick glance toward Miss Lombardo, Dominic said, "Look, I couldn't care less about this thing — " Then he pointed at Mr.

Frye. "But let me tell *you* something! First of all, *you* are full of it, 'cause this ain't about money! They don't need your money! As a matter of fact, they could probably do Sing and never cost you a cent!"

Go home, Dominic, Hannah wanted to say. Haven't you done enough — ?

"Mr. Leonetti, Mr. Scarpatti!" Dominic called out to two men in the crowd. "You guys are retired cops. You think you could get some more guys and take care of security?"

The two men nodded.

"What about a clean-up crew?" Dominic continued.

Several people raised their hands. The room began to buzz again.

Hannah felt Dominic's eyes fixing on her. She turned away, furious. Out of the corner of her eye, she noticed her mother looking from her to Dominic, wondering what was going on.

"Just a minute!" came Mr. Frye's voice. "Order!"

But Dominic plowed right on. "And they're going to need some material — wood for the sets. . . ."

"You'll get all the wood you need!" Hannah was amazed to see old Mr. Abaldi of Abaldi's Lumber step forward.

A cheer went up all around.

Now Dominic was walking closer to Hannah. "And paint!" he yelled, practically in her ear. "Who's gonna throw in the paint?"

Murray raised his hand, along with some of the others. For the first time, Hannah saw Nathan smile at Murray.

Too bad none of this was going to work. Play the hero, you sleazeball, she thought. Get everyone else in this community to trust you so you can pull the wool over their eyes. But I'm not falling for it again.

Hannah stood up and ran out of the room.

Dominic looked after her, feeling a pit in his stomach. To his right, Mrs. Tucci was yelling out, "We need fabric! I can handle that! Who else? Jerry? Sol?"

It was working. The show might really happen. What more does she want? Dominic thought.

The place was a madhouse. "Shut up!" Mr. Frye screamed at the top of his lungs. "*SHUT UP!*"

Suddenly the room fell silent. A renewed hope was in everyone's eyes — along with a giddiness that made them all look like kids again. They gazed up at Mr. Frye breathlessly, with triumphant expectation.

He stared back at them. Then, in a firm, flat voice, he gave his final answer.

"No."

Chapter 14

Miss Lombardo blew the steam off her Styrofoam cup of coffee. Outside the pizza parlor, the drizzle made the streets glow with the reflection of the cars' headlights. After the meeting this evening, she felt as if her mind had gone blank.

"You know, Theresa," Mr. Marowitz said, "for twenty-one years I've been a good administrator. Policy man. Nose to the grindstone. For what? So now they come to me and tell me they're going to close my school."

Miss Lombardo stared off into the distance. "I remember my last year at Bay Ridge, that final Sing. It was wonderful. And it was important. We worked *so* hard. I remember the sets . . . and the choreography! Do you know? I think I saved my costume."

Mr. Marowitz smiled in response.

"And we were a family, for one night," Miss Lombardo went on. "And I just wanted *them* to feel. . . ." She exhaled. Somehow, when she thought about Central, her thoughts jumbled up inside of her. "These kids . . . they didn't care —

about anything! And I come back in here, Miss Rootin'-Tootin' . . . and some of them actually got excited. . . ."

Her voice trailed off. It was painful to say what was underneath all this. "I . . . I feel like such a fraud."

"I'll tell you one thing," Mr. Marowitz said. "I've worked *within* this system for so long — I can certainly figure out ways to work outside it. And no stuffy Elliot Frye from the Board of Education is going to stop us from giving those kids one final Sing!"

His words gave Miss Lombardo a lift. But he was probably just blowing off steam. "You could lose your job, you know," she said.

Mr. Marowitz gave her a firm look. "This *is* my job."

Adjusting his collar, the man looked at his checklist as he walked down the hall. His sharp footsteps echoed against the fading walls of the empty school. He cast a glance toward the auditorium doors and made a note. Then he walked away toward the southern end of the building.

Inside the auditorium, Hannah held her breath. The entire senior class stood frozen, their hammers and paintbrushes poised. Everyone waited for Naomi's signal.

The man's footsteps began to fade away. A moment later, Naomi finally pulled her face away from the crack in the auditorium door. She quickly turned into the room.

"Go!"

Instantly they all swung into action — building sets, carrying lights back and forth, rehearsing lines, singing songs. Hannah went around inspecting everything. As usual, her *other* Sing leader wasn't around to help.

"That's supposed to be blue!" she called up to a girl on a ladder, who was painting one of the flats.

"Dominic said *black*," the girl replied.

"Do you see him here anywhere? No! And *I* don't want you painting the sky black!" She walked on, consulting the Sing rehearsal schedule in her hand. Then she announced, "Everybody in the Candle scene meet in the alley behind Murray Bloom's hardware store at seven-thirty!"

A tiny *tip-tip-tip* noise caught her attention. She looked down to see someone tapping a nail with gentle mini-strokes. "Cyril, what are you doing?"

Cyril looked up defensively. "If Mr. Frye catches us — "

Hannah shook her head. "Look — " She put her hand to her mouth and let out a long, piercing whistle. All activity stopped. When she saw that she had everyone's attention, she spoke softly but firmly.

"Look, we can build these sets here. Other than that, we'll do everything away from school. And we're not going to be stopped. Not by Mr. Frye — not by any of his goons. Mr. Marowitz has put himself on the line for us. All that's left for us to do is take those sophomores and juniors and wipe the floor with them!"

Swept away by the spirit that she was creating, Hannah suddenly threw her head back and screamed, "SENIOR VICTORY!"

A roar went up all around the auditorium. "VICTORY!"

Nathan's feet slapped the pavement as he ran down the street. There was no way he could hide the huge paper bag he was holding. If anyone caught him now, anyone *important*. . . .

He stopped outside the door of a nondescript building. Shooting his eyes right and left one last time, he knocked.

Behind him, the blinds in a first-floor window lifted. A pair of suspicious eyes peered out.

A second later, the door opened and a hand reached out to pull Nathan inside.

Nathan found himself back where he'd started — in a dance studio, where the secret underclass Sing preparations were taking place. He looked around with a sigh of relief.

Passing around coffee and donuts from his bag, Nathan bounced to the beat of Blade's band, which was practicing a number with Zena. Next to the band, the school janitor helped a group of students and parents assemble set pieces. In one corner, some half-costumed tap dancers stumbled through their routine, while beside them a committee rushed to finish their costumes. Everyone looked completely exhausted.

But one voice was louder than all the rest —

Mrs. Devere's. She stormed through the room, shouting directions, answering questions, changing things here and there. Her brow was furrowed with frustration. Things weren't going as well as she wanted. She stopped in front of the band, where Ari was arguing about the music.

She listened a moment, shook her head, and then shouted over the noise, "People . . . hold the work there!"

A few students turned to listen.

"People — I said HOLD THE WORK!"

At that, the music stopped and all activity ground to a halt.

Mrs. Devere's eyes were like lasers as she looked around the studio. "I think we'd better get something straight right here and now: Either we are going to make history, or we are going to *be* history." She focused on a group of students. "You think you're tired now? Well, you don't know what tired is! You *all* think you've been working hard? Well, *they*'ve been working harder!"

She gestured over her shoulder, and everyone knew whom she meant — the seniors. She glared at Ari and the band. "You think you've got a winning show? Well, you'd better pick up that tempo right now, or we might as well *aaaall* pack up our bags and go home! Now try it again!"

She pumped her hands in a fast rhythm, and the band followed.

And then, to Nathan's delight, Mrs. Devere began to sing! She took his breath away. Mrs. Devere had been there just as long as the rest of them, but she threw herself into the song with the energy of ten people.

She finished in a frenzy that made James Brown look lazy. And when the echo of the last crashing chord resounded through the room, everyone's mouth was hanging open.

In the stunned silence, Mrs. Devere calmly walked up to Ari and put her finger on his chest. "And *that* is how you pay the rent."

Immediately the sounds of work started again — but louder, more intense. Nathan felt exhilarated.

And that's when the whispering started. Nathan caught it happening out of the corner of his eye, but he had no idea what was going on — until Ari's voice rang out above the others.

"Our paint?" he said, his eyes widening in disbelief. "The seniors stole our paint?" Ari was outraged — and so was everyone else within his earshot.

Including Nathan. He knew it had become more than just a contest. It was a war.

Chapter 15

"All *riiight*, Hannah!" Denise Popolato said. She and the other girls had just worked through Hannah's dance combination. All the weeks of changes and mistakes were paying off. The dance looked fantastic — not to mention the glitzy, sexy costumes.

Hannah felt a rush of triumph. It's going to work, she said to herself. Who needs the Italian Wonderboy, after all?

"Okay, take five and we'll do it again," Hannah said. She smiled and walked away, glancing at all the activity around her.

This empty warehouse was perfect, she thought. High ceilings, huge floor — and far away from the school. They were so lucky one of the seniors' fathers owned it. He'd even volunteered to drive the sets to the school on his flatbed truck.

She smiled. It sure beat that stupid little dance studio the underclassmen were using.

Over by the far wall, a few of the students

were assembling an enormous set. Hannah watched in admiration as it took shape.

She wondered why three of them were wearing hoods over their heads — and why they were running past the set without looking at it. Hannah followed them with her eyes. They headed straight for a stack of paint cans.

Just then, a voice boomed out, "Underclassmen! Sabotage! They're stealing our paint! Get 'em!"

The three thieves bolted for the door. One of them had managed to pick up two open cans of paint.

Hannah ran after them, joined by an angry horde of seniors. The underclassmen were way ahead; there was no way they were going to be caught. Frantically, the one with the cans of paint glanced over his shoulder — and his hood fell off.

Ari Thermopoulos, Hannah said to herself. I might have known.

Ari raced for the front door, just ahead of his pursuers. Had he been looking ahead, he would have seen Mr. Marowitz coming through the door.

But he didn't.

Thud — splashhhh! It was a direct hit. Mr. Marowitz was covered head-to-toe with paint.

Everyone in the warehouse stopped in his or her tracks. Ari's mouth fell open in horror.

Hannah waited for the explosion. She knew Sing was hanging on a thread; without Mr. Marowitz's support, they were finished.

There *was* an explosion — but not from Mr.

Marowitz. Clutching her stomach, Miss Lombardo suddenly burst into uncontrollable laughter.

The seniors all stood there, not knowing what to do. All eyes were on Mr. Marowitz.

But he didn't yell at Ari at all. In fact, he didn't say a word. He merely reached down and picked up one of the cans. Then, calmly, he walked over to the giggling Miss Lombardo — and poured the rest of the contents over her head.

Everyone backed away in shock. The underclassmen disappeared out the door.

In the midst of the horrified silence, a chuckle bubbled up from Mr. Marowitz. Then another. In an instant, both he and Miss Lombardo were roaring with laughter.

And relief washed through the room as the entire senior class joined in.

That night Hannah trudged wearily home. The rehearsals, plus all the shifts at the diner, were finally beginning to take their toll — but it was all worth it. Underneath all the fatigue, she knew there was something to be proud of.

At the bottom of the front stoop to her house, she reached into her bag for her keys. Even *that* seemed like an effort. It would feel so good to sink into bed —

Suddenly she felt herself being grabbed from behind.

"*Auugh — !*" A stifled scream was all she could manage as a hand closed firmly over her mouth.

Chapter 16

She tried to whirl around but her attacker had her in a viselike grip.

"Hannah!"

It was Dominic! Hannah lurched from side to side, but he held tight and pulled her away from the stairs. "I know you don't wanna see me, you don't wanna hear from me," he said. "But there's something I had to do."

He held up an envelope that had a watch wrapped around it. "That's my Rolex. It's worth a lot; I don't know how much. And there's cash in the envelope — almost two hundred dollars. It's all I got."

But Hannah could only see red. As he slowly released her, she felt hatred racing through her like a brushfire. "And what's this for?" she hissed. "I thought you were clean, Dominic."

"Look, just 'cause I wanna help out doesn't mean I did nothing. Let's just suppose that I know these guys who knew about your robbery — just suppose — and I get to feeling bad about — "

Hannah smacked him in the chest with the envelope. "It was four thousand dollars, you fool! Don't try to buy me off with some wristwatch — "

"It's a Rolex! Look at it — "

" —'cause that four thousand dollars broke my mother's back. Insurance ain't going to pay it, we're not going to make it, and we don't have it. But I bet *you* know who does!"

She spun away, but Dominic pulled her back. "I don't got it, Hannah — I swear! What if I pay you back, a little at a time? Say one hundred a month — "

"I hear your brother does okay for himself. You want to help? Get the money from him!" With that, Hannah yanked herself out of his grip and turned toward the stairs.

"Hannah," Dominic pleaded. "Hannah! You don't know Freddy. That kind of money — he'll *kill* me!"

Hannah turned and gave him a poisonous glare. "And what do you want from me — tears?"

Dominic had no answer for that. And Hannah wasn't going to give him the chance to dream one up. Setting her jaw, she walked up the stairs and opened the front door.

As Hannah went inside and Dominic slumped away, neither of them saw the window on the second floor closing. And neither of them saw the look of dismay on Rosie's face as she backed away into her bedroom and let the curtains fall in front of her.

The next day, as Miss Lombardo cleaned out her belongings in the teacher's lounge, she felt on the verge of tears. She was glad Mr. Marowitz was there; it would have been too depressing to do this alone.

The school had that musty, late-evening feeling. Only the occasional whoosh of a vacuum cleaner broke the eerie silence. Sighing, Miss Lombardo shook her head at all the books strewn on her desk. "Where do all of these come from?" she said. "I never studied them, I never even got to teach half of them." She chuckled. "Don't we start out with high hopes. . . ."

"We do," Mr. Marowitz said with a shrug. "And then we do what we can."

Miss Lombardo stacked the books in a cardboard box until she heard Mr. Marowitz's voice behind her.

"Close your eyes."

A smile crept across her face. "Why?"

"Just close your eyes."

She did — and she felt something settling gently around her neck. She opened her eyes.

It was some sort of medal. "What . . . ?" Puzzled, she looked at Mr. Marowitz, whose smiling face was now inches away from hers.

"The kids gave it to me," Mr. Marowitz said. "Just before I made principal. It's for being the most inspirational teacher."

Miss Lombardo felt herself blushing. "Oh, stop! I can't take — "

"No, no. Keep it. You've inspired me on more than one occasion."

She touched the medal, flattered and a little embarrassed. But when she looked at him, she knew he hadn't told her everything. His eyes were continuing the conversation. They were saying something that hadn't been said to Theresa Lombardo in a long, long time. Something that could only be answered one way.

She would never have thought that a kiss in the teachers' lounge would have felt so thrilling.

When their lips parted, Miss Lombardo turned away shyly and picked up her box of books. "Thank you . . ." she said, fingering her medal. "Good night."

"Good night," Mr. Marowitz answered softly.

She stood in the doorway, not wanting to leave. For a moment, she struggled for words.

But all that came out was "Yeah . . . well . . . good night."

As she walked away, the last thing she saw was the expression on Mr. Marowitz's face. He was beaming.

Crassssh! Hannah plopped a loaded bus tray down near the dishwasher. She was still in the clothes she had worn to school; after a late, sweaty rehearsal, it just seemed ridiculous to change into her uniform. Besides, the diner was already closed.

"Those rehearsals keep running so late, you're

going to be showing up *after* I've locked up," Rosie said pointedly. In front of her was a stack of mail she still hadn't opened. She slid her finger under the flap of an envelope. "Not that it matters anymore. Murray's accountant, Bernie Schisgal, looked over my books today and told me that I ought to put this place on the market as soon as — "

Hannah waited for the end of the sentence, but it didn't come. She turned to see her mother pulling something from an envelope. Rosie's mouth hung open in amazement.

It was cash. A huge stack of it.

Hannah rushed over to her and grabbed it out of her hand. He did it, she said to herself, staring at the wad of neatly packed twenties. That low-life actually did it.

Rosie looked at her daughter through narrowed eyes. "Do you know something about this?"

"What?" Hannah said, distracted.

"What do you know about this?"

When Hannah didn't answer, Rosie snatched the money back. "I've been such an idiot," she said. "You knew where this money was all the time, didn't you?"

Hannah couldn't lie, but how could she explain why she hadn't told on Dominic? Even *she* didn't understand why!

Rosie's eyes flashed with hostility. "And you sat there and let some stupid punk kid destroy our lives and — "

"His name is Dominic. And you don't know him."

"Oh? And you do?"

"The money is back," Hannah said quietly.

Rosie exploded. "That boy is scum! He is garbage! And when you take his side against your family, you are no better!"

Hannah slapped the money out of Rosie's hand. It spilled onto the floor. "Is that what you think of me? Are you so bitter and disappointed that *that's* how I look to you?"

"Listen, if I was living your life — "

"You are *not* living my life!" Hannah screamed. "And I don't *ever* want to be living yours!"

She stormed away, slamming the kitchen door behind her.

Chapter 17

Boom . . . boom . . . boom. . . .

Miss Lombardo stopped walking when she heard the pounding beat. She wasn't sure what to expect going home this late — but rock music from the old bus depot seemed pretty strange.

There was a light on inside, and the front door was open. She hesitated a moment, then decided to peek in.

And there, next to a blaring portable tape deck, was Dominic. With savage energy, he worked through a dance step, over and over. The muscles in his arms glistened with sweat as they slashed the musty air, and his face radiated a ferocious, restless fury.

Tentatively she walked inside. The thing that struck her most was his *anger*. The depot seemed too small to contain it. It seemed to roar out of him, bouncing off the walls, threatening to tear the roof off.

Silently, she leaned against the wall and watched in awe.

When he finally turned off the tape, she called out to him, "A person could get mugged out here at this hour."

Dominic jumped backward. He shot her a startled look.

"Where have you been?" Miss Lombardo continued, walking toward him. "Why don't you come around?"

"I've been busy working with my brother," Dominic answered coolly. "Family business."

Miss Lombardo nodded. "There's a whole family of people who want you to come back to Sing. You've got a lot of friends — "

"I don't need friends! I always got plenty of friends!"

"Oh, yeah? Who? You know, most of these kids didn't know your name before this year. You almost got through high school without anybody knowing who you are. Some trick!"

Dominic narrowed his eyes. "I'm gonna tell you something. My brother Freddy — he's the only one who cares about me. More than just about anybody!"

He turned away from her and flipped on the tape. Ignoring her, he started dancing again.

But instead of leaving, Miss Lombardo watched him carefully and stood next to him. She struck a few poses, trying to copy his movements. It wasn't a great imitation, but she knew she'd gotten the essence.

Dominic stared at her. "Where'd you learn to do that?"

"I watched you."

"Come on. . . ."

Miss Lombardo knew she had his attention. "Rehearsals are going well," she said, dropping a heavy hint. "Especially under the circumstances. The seniors might even win."

"So?" Dominic said angrily.

"So . . . how does the rest of the combination go?"

"There's no more."

"Sure there is."

"I don't know!" Dominic snapped. "There's no more!"

"There is! I was watching you!"

"Look, you want everybody singing and dancing all the time — that's your problem."

"Oh, and you don't got any problems?"

Dominic wheeled around. He stood over her, his eyes burning with rage. "You got it so perfect? You got so much to look forward to? No husband, no kids, no job, no life? You're a real winner!"

Miss Lombardo felt as if she'd been smacked in the face. She turned away, dumbfounded.

Dominic fell silent, too. For a long, awkward moment, the two of them just stood there.

"I never hurt you . . ." Miss Lombardo finally said, her voice practically a whisper.

"Go home, lady," Dominic muttered.

"You are so young," Miss Lombardo replied. "One mistake doesn't ruin your life — unless you let it."

Dominic stared at the ground. Behind his tough, angry features, Miss Lombardo could see something else. He was in pain. For the first time, she sensed that they had something in common.

She leaned down and turned the tape recorder back on. The music began again, and Dominic looked away. Miss Lombardo began to sway to the music. She looked at him, hoping he'd join.

But he just stood still, with his back to her.

The music swelled. Miss Lombardo's moves became surer, more dramatic. She let loose a dance kick — inches from Dominic's face.

Dominic spun around, his eyes glowing fiercely. "Where'd you learn to do that?" he demanded.

"I watched you," Miss Lombardo teased. "And I used to take dance lessons, but that was a long time ago."

The contest was on. With a sudden, sharp snap of his leg, Dominic responded with a kick that made Miss Lombardo's look amateurish. After each move Miss Lombardo made, he followed with one that was sharper, hotter. Slowly they began circling one another, their bodies taut with pent-up energy.

Then, as if finally giving in to a trust that neither wanted to admit, they began to dance together. In a whirl of motion, they flew across the bus depot floor. They suddenly found themselves among hulking pieces of machinery. With a mischievous smile, Miss Lombardo ducked behind one of them, out of sight. Dominic darted behind another, and they both found themselves in a giddy kind of hide-and-seek.

Finally, with a reluctant smile, Dominic grabbed her and lifted her off the ground into a soaring leap. They moved to the middle of the floor, working off each other flawlessly, as the music soared to a climax.

At the sound of the last, crashing chords, they ended the dance face-to-face — and Miss Lombardo saw something in Dominic's eyes she'd never expected to see.

Respect.

And what's more, she felt it for him. All this time, she'd been trying to get through to Dominic, to *teach* him. She never suspected that he had something to teach her — a way to shake out the anger and misery that had built up inside her.

It was a wonderful lesson. As she collapsed with exhaustion against a nearby post, she felt light-hearted with joy.

Dominic walked over to her and reached down. She took his hand and rose to her feet. Together, for the first time since they'd met, they shared a smile.

Click. Behind them, the tape stopped in the middle of a song. Miss Lombardo looked over her shoulder. Standing over the tape was a young, dark-haired man she'd never seen before. He began walking toward them, his eyes blazing with a murderous intensity.

Dominic stiffened with panic. He let go of Miss Lombardo's hand and ran.

The dark-haired guy took off after him. "You

little toad," he spat out. "You back-stabbing little toad!"

The hatred in his voice cut the air like a dagger. Miss Lombardo backed away in shock. She stood helplessly as their footsteps sent ugly, jagged echoes through the depot.

Suddenly the echoes stopped. Dominic was in a corner. He whirled around, his face lined with fear. "Freddy! Freddy, listen!" he pleaded. "I couldn't go through with it!"

Freddy barely let him finish. His fist connected with Dominic's jaw, sending him flying against the wall. Dominic cried out in pain. Freddy punched him again . . . and again. Before long his arms and legs were pumping in a merciless rage.

Like a battered rag doll, Dominic finally crumpled to the ground. The depot became silent again, except for the sound of Freddy's heavy breathing. Miss Lombardo felt sick to her stomach.

After a final, violent kick, Freddy turned around. And as he strode back through the depot, his icy glare avoided Miss Lombardo.

She ran to Dominic. Her heart skipped a beat when she saw the bloody mess his brother had left.

She dropped to her knees. Then, gently, she lifted him off the ground and cradled him in her arms.

Chapter 18

Thump.

Mr. Marowitz stopped in his tracks. He gave Naomi a quizzical look. Up until now, everything had been going much better than expected. It was already the Friday before Sing, and so far the Board of Education hadn't suspected a thing.

Thump.

But that noise in the auditorium made his heart sink. "Come on," he said. He and Naomi ran across the hallway and through the auditorium door.

There, Mr. Marowitz saw that his worst fear had come true. A group of workmen was unbolting seats and pulling them out. One of the men from the Board of Education stood over them supervising.

"My God," Mr. Marowitz muttered. "Not today — of all days!" He marched down the aisle, calling out, "*What* are you doing?"

The Board of Education man looked up. "Getting a jump on Monday morning."

"At five-thirty on a Friday? Isn't it about weekend time for you?"

"Not if I can empty this place ahead of schedule."

"Well, *I'm* in no hurry. . . ." Mr. Marowitz turned and shouted to the workmen: "Excuse me . . . *excuse me!* Please put those down!"

"Now just a minute!" the Board of Education man protested. "I'll have to call Mr. Frye!"

"Look, if Elliot Frye wants these seats out of here, he can come down here himself and pull them out with his teeth."

The workmen stood bewildered as Mr. Marowitz ran up to them. But he knew how to handle them — exactly the same way he handled them when they were students at Central.

With his toughest inner-city principal snarl, he calmly said, "Put those back — every single one of them."

And just as he expected, not one of them dared disobey.

As Mrs. Tucci opened the back door of the kitchen, the Saturday afternoon sun streamed in. She paused in the doorway, holding a large, flat sheet cake. ". . . you woulda loved it last night, Rosie," she said. "There was kids and parents all working late, and about three in the morning, Carol Hershkowitz and me got up on the stage and did the finale from the 1959 show — and we remembered it! We was laughing so hard! Then someone reminds us that this is the last one, and ohhh. . . ." She shook her head with a mixture of sorrow and disgust.

Rosie nodded, pretending not to be interested.

"People's saying that Hannah did great with the seniors," Mrs. Tucci continued.

This time Rosie's ears perked up. "Is that so?"

"She doesn't tell you?"

Rosie shrugged.

"Well," Mrs. Tucci said, licking icing from her fingers, "they're all working very hard."

Hannah quietly walked into the kitchen, without either woman noticing her. As usual, Mrs. Tucci was doing something constructive for the underclass Sing. It made Hannah hurt inside that Rosie hadn't even helped out at any of the senior rehearsals.

Mrs. Tucci leaned in from the back door. "Rosie, you're an angel, as always. I'm gonna get this over to the school." She gave Rosie a kiss on the cheek. "I'll see you there tonight."

"Oh, I don't know," Rosie said distractedly.

"Rosie, don't talk nonsense." With a laugh, she left the diner.

As Rosie turned back into the kitchen, Hannah walked toward her. Their eyes met briefly, but Rosie said nothing.

Hannah held out a pair of tickets. "I brought you your tickets," she said. "It's at seven-thirty."

"You sold out?" Rosie said.

"Packed. We set a record. At least we're going out with a bang."

Rosie looked away. Her face showed absolutely no emotion. Hannah nodded meaninglessly and shuffled her feet. She couldn't think of anything to say. Finally, after a long silence, she repeated, "I brought you your tickets."

"Maybe you want to give these to somebody who can use them," Rosie said nonchalantly.

"You got other seats?"

"Other seats? No, no. I just got a lot of things I got to do here and back at the house, I decided." With that, she turned her back and began busying herself around the kitchen. "But you have a good time."

Hannah felt her jaw go slack. She couldn't believe what her mother was doing. If she stayed in the kitchen one more minute, she was going to explode.

She turned on her heels. In a fit of rage, she slammed the tickets on the counter and stormed out.

Chapter 19

"Heyyyyy, how're ya doin'?"

Mr. Marowitz nodded politely and shook hands with Margie Green's father. "Fine. Excuse me." He dodged through the crowd, carrying an unbolted seat back toward the auditorium. This was it — the night that the Board of Education couldn't stop. The forty-first annual Sing.

The show was minutes away from curtain time and the lobby was packed. But Mr. Marowitz was determined not to let anyone sit down until the last removed seat was put back. He reached for the auditorium door — but before he could open it, a voice stopped him.

"Phil, what on earth are you doing?"

He spun around to see Mr. Frye pushing his way through the throng, his face crimson with fury. "Do you think that I give orders just to hear myself talk?"

Mr. Marowitz had no time to argue. "Elliot," he said, "you don't want me to answer that."

At the other end of the hallway, Mr. Marowitz

spotted Mrs. Tucci, fingering a key ring and watching Mr. Frye. Suddenly she ran toward him, waving her arms over her head.

"Mr. Marowitz! Oh, thank God, Mr. Marowitz!" she called out breathlessly. She stepped between him and Mr. Frye. Lowering her voice to a whisper, she continued, "I don't wanna cause a panic, but there seems to be a small fire in the basement."

Mr. Marowitz dropped the chair. He and Mrs. Tucci sped down the nearest set of stairs, followed close behind by Mr. Frye.

Mrs. Tucci led them through the basement. They wound through a maze of dark hallways lined with storage rooms. "Down here!" she finally called over her shoulder.

Huffing and puffing, Mr. Frye stayed at Mr. Marowitz's heels. "I will see to it that you *never* work in the educational system again!" he yelled. "Where *is* that fire?"

A few yards ahead, Mrs. Tucci stopped in front of a storeroom door. As Mr. Frye and Mr. Marowitz arrived, she flung the door open.

The two men immediately poked their heads in — and with a strong shove, Mrs. Tucci pushed Mr. Frye inside. She slammed the door behind him.

"Go!" she commanded, pushing Mr. Marowitz back the way they came. "The fire is out!"

Mr. Marowitz took off like a shot, shaking with laughter as he ran. Behind him, he heard Mr. Frye banging on the door and shouting.

"Elliot Frye," came Mrs. Tucci's voice, "you

were a pimply, four-eyed dork in twelfth grade, and now you're a four-eyed dork with a bad hairpiece!"

Stanley lumbered through the basement. He couldn't believe the underclassmen had hidden five hundred pounds of the seniors' dry ice. Behind him, half the football team raced from door to door, frantically testing doorknobs.

"This is crazy!" one of them yelled. "I don't even know what dry ice looks like!"

"Like ice!" Stanley called out. "Only . . . uh . . . dry!" He skidded to a stop in front of the boys' bathroom. Smoke was billowing out from underneath the doorway.

He yanked the door open, sending a thick cloud of steam into the hallway. "It's in the *toilets?*"

Stanley raced blindly into the bathroom, just as one of his friends shouted, "Hey, watch it! These floors are like glass!"

Too late. With a *whissssh* and a resounding crunch, Stanley slipped and landed headfirst on the tiled floor.

"One minute to curtain, Nathan!" Mrs. Devere said.

Nathan looked at his hands in horror. They were both clutching the curtain rope — but he couldn't feel them!

"Did you *hear* me, Nathan?"

On the darkened stage, juniors and sophomores bustled around, fixing flats, rehearsing movements, adjusting lights. But Nathan didn't notice any of it. He was staring at his knuckles, which had turned white. It's rigor mortis, he told himself. And I'm not even dead yet.

"NA-A-A-TH-A-A-N!"

With a jolt, Nathan yanked on the curtains.

"No, not *now*! Wait for the signal!"

He looked sheepishly over his shoulder to see Mrs. Devere staring at him. Pulling his hands away from the curtain, he exercised his fingers. They were fine. A little tight, but fine.

And over near the light board, Zena gave him a furtive glance and giggled.

Well, Nathan thought, his face turning red, at least she noticed me.

"Okay, *now*, Nathan, *now*!"

Nathan felt his stomach leap into his mouth. He gripped the curtain rope again. After all the sneaking around, after all the fights and sleepless nights, Sing was really going to happen!

With a strong, confident motion, he pulled open the curtain.

Chapter 20

" 'Oh, Juliet, thou beautiful rose. . . .' "

Nathan tingled with excitement. It wasn't so hard being onstage, after all — especially if all you had to do was stand still and blend into the background. He listened attentively as Zena Ward and David Hershkowitz recited Romeo and Juliet's lines.

But he couldn't keep his eyes away from the audience. Every seat was filled, and people even stood two-deep in the back. Some of these students would normally never even let themselves be seen in school after-hours. Like the group of tough guys who sat with their arms crossed in the balcony — wearing sunglasses!

Just then his eyes were drawn to a strange sight — an empty seat. He felt his heart sink.

The seat was next to Murray. Rosie was nowhere in sight.

" 'O canst not love me as I wouldst,' " David Hershkowitz continued, his voice projecting loudly, " 'for my parents do forbid it. I am much troubled.' "

Zena turned to him. "Trouble?" she said. "Romeo, I'm gonna tell you what trouble is — it's all those *thee*s and *thou*s. And the fact that your momma and papa don't want to see us together. Honey, let's face it — they're too uptight! Matter of fact, this whole *town* is too uptight!"

Suddenly she stepped forward and ripped off her costume. Underneath it was a wild and funky street outfit.

A howl of delight went up from the crowd. Zena began to sing in the spotlight, as the stage beneath her fell into darkness. On cue, Nathan hurried off the stage and watched from the wings.

Zena hopped over to the edge of the balcony and hung out over the stage below, clutching the railing. Just then she let go of the railing and fell. Nathan held his breath.

But just as planned, she landed in the waiting arms of a group of dancers below. Bright lights washed across the stage, revealing a set designed to look like a street. A real *Brooklyn* street — pizza joint, taxicabs, and even a building that looked like Brooklyn Central High.

The crowd roared again. Zena began to dance, slinking from one side of the stage to the other. She whirled around to a part of the set that was built to look like a shop. She picked out a pair of shoes and put them on.

Then, as she leaped to center stage, the lights dimmed. Zena danced as if she were on fire. And the audience went wild as her shoes lit up in the dark!

Nathan could feel the walls shaking as the whole place rocked to the beat of Zena's song. He thought his cheeks would break from smiling so much, and as he looked around him in the wings, he realized everyone felt the same way.

Well, *almost* everyone. With each scream from the audience, Cecelia Tucci seemed to sink deeper and deeper into a smouldering rage. Ari tried to calm her down as she paced back and forth.

Nathan couldn't help but laugh. He peeked out into the audience to see that even the seven Sing judges were bopping in time to the song.

He could smell an underclass victory.

"Yeeeouch!" Unheard by anyone else in the building, Mr. Frye stubbed his toe in the dark. He cursed the box that was in his way, even though he was glad it was there.

It was yet another one he could stack against the wall. Another few feet closer to the high window that glowed with the light from outside.

Hannah was hysterical with nerves. The sounds of the screaming audience could be heard all the way in the gym. Whatever the underclassmen were doing, it was *good*. And if Hannah couldn't pull this thing together now, she'd never have another chance.

Off to one side of the gym, a group of seniors tried to revive Stanley, but he was out cold. Why couldn't it have been someone with a smaller part? Hannah thought. Frantically she and Miss Lombardo tried to restage the finale. As they called out instructions, seniors dressed in flowing robes moved around obediently.

"Who stands here?" Naomi called out, pointing to an empty spot in the group's lineup.

"Stanley!" one of the boys called out.

Everyone began to talk at once, yelling out suggestions. Hannah turned to Miss Lombardo and shouted over the din, "I'm going to go get Clarissa. Maybe we can cut the music down and skip over Stanley's part!"

She tore across the gym, hoping the plan would work. If Clarissa could replace the middle section with a vamp —

She pulled open the door, started to run through — and stopped herself just short of a collision with someone who was walking in. Actually, *limping* in was more the word for it.

She gasped in horror as she looked up into Dominic's swollen, bloody face.

Chapter 21

Hannah tried to speak, but she felt the words catch in her throat. "What are you — are you okay? I . . . I was worried about you."

A powerful feeling welled up inside of her — a feeling she didn't want to admit, *couldn't* admit.

Dominic's eyes penetrated deep into hers, as if he could read her mind. The old toughness was still there, but underneath it was something new. Something gentle and vulnerable that made her shiver.

His lips curled into a tiny, pained half smile. "Ah, it ain't too bad," he said. "Doctor says I'll be able to think again in about two weeks."

Hannah smiled. Before she could say anything, an excited voice called out, "It's Dominic!"

In seconds Dominic was surrounded by seniors. He winced in pain as they hugged him, kissed him, slapped him on the back. Their voices overlapped as they tried to fill him in.

"Stanley hit his head and passed out!"

"We gotta rewrite the show, get somebody to do his part — "

"Yeah, but who knows his lines?"

"Who knows the dances?"

"Who knows the songs?"

Suddenly they all stopped. One by one, their eyes lit up. And their heads all turned in the same direction — toward Dominic.

Dominic backed away. He looked from Hannah to Miss Lombardo. "Ohhh, no," he said, shaking his head. "Lombardo, I seen that look before. . . ."

At that moment the auditorium was quiet. Onstage, the underclassmen were acting out Romeo's and Juliet's deaths. Mourners filed into an open tomb in a graveyard, where Zena and David lay on concrete slabs.

Nathan swallowed hard. He knew the next part was Cecelia's song. He looked over to see her pacing back and forth. Her rhinestone-studded outfit twinkled in the dim backstage lights. I don't believe she's going to wear that thing, Nathan thought. It had absolutely no relation to anything on the stage — the period costumes *or* the flashy street outfits.

Cecelia cast an agitated glance out to the stage. Behind her, her two backup dancers giggled with nervous anticipation.

Ari paced along with her. "They aren't going to know what hit them!" he said. "This act is brilliant! Break a leg, babe!"

"Don't bother me with that stuff now!"

"Why?"

Just then Cecelia heard her cue. She wheeled around at Ari. "Because I have to go out there and save this show!"

She took a deep breath and walked onto the stage. Excitedly, her two backups followed — and ran right into Ari.

"Sorry, kids," Ari said, not moving an inch, "this trio is now a solo."

Alone, Cecelia walked into Romeo and Juliet's tomb, as the mourners left the stage. She watched the last one place a rose near the dead lovers' bodies.

Then she turned to the audience. "Poor Romeo and Juliet!" she announced. "So sad. That's the trouble with death — it's so depressing. . . ."

Blade began conducting the band, and Cecelia started to sing.

She lifted up Zena's and David's hands and tried to join them, but they fell lifelessly to the ground. Behind her, dancers dressed as skeletons began to rise from the graveyard. As Cecelia sang, they broke into a tap dance.

One by one, more skeletons popped out of graves. Joining the others, they formed a chorus line of the undead.

Like a cheerleader in a funeral parlor, Cecelia did a series of high kicks and splits, a smile frozen on her face.

Nathan's jaw dropped. It was even worse than he'd expected.

In the wings, Ari was ready to burst with pride.

Next to him, Mrs. Devere raised a wary eyebrow to Mr. Marowitz. "Mmm, *mmm*," she said under her breath. "Is there no end to her talent?"

Suddenly a puff of smoke burst on the stage. Fallen leaves swirled all around, and in the middle of it all a new character appeared — a middle-aged adult in a gravedigger costume.

The audience howled with approval at the sight of Louie, the school janitor!

Puffing on his cigar, Louie picked up Zena and David and brought them to the front of the stage. They remained limp as he propped them up for the final chorus of the song.

A pall fell over the audience. Nathan could see people gaping at the sight of the two "corpses" shoved to the side as the dance went on behind them.

The band hit the final chords, to gales of laughter from the audience.

Nathan cringed. He could tell by the crushed look on Cecelia's face that she realized they were laughing *at* her, not with her.

She stormed into the wings, where Ari was applauding wildly. When he saw the angry look on her face, he reached out his arms to comfort her.

Cecelia let her eyes meet his — just long enough to take aim. She hauled off and belted him in the face.

As she stalked off to the dressing room, Mrs. Devere followed her with her eyes. Then she turned to Mr. Marowitz and shrugged. "Just like

I always say, sometimes you just kick 'em in the rear!"

The words flashed before Dominic's eyes. He mouthed them over and over again, trying to memorize the lines. Every few seconds he felt a blinding shot of pain as several girls applied makeup to cover his bruises.

Around him, the senior class reacted to the news about Louie. Angrily they shouted in protest.

"It's against the rules!" insisted one of the makeup girls. "We're supposed to do it on our own!" Dominic winced as she poked his face to emphasize her point.

"And . . . AND. . . ." Miss Lombardo tried to make herself heard over the noise. " . . . the judges ruled that because Louie is *not* a faculty member, they *are* going to allow it!"

Now the shouts became bloodthirsty. "We'll kill them!" someone screamed. "Senior victory!" another voice piped up.

"Now just remember," Miss Lombardo continued, "we've got a long show. *We cannot afford to be penalized for going overtime!* So keep up the pace!"

With renewed energy, the senior class plunged into final preparations.

And on the dark, empty sidewalk outside the school building, a lone figure moved. A figure crawling out of a basement window, his face twisted with vengeance.

Chapter 22

Murray hadn't moved this fast in years. But then again, he hadn't felt this strongly about anything in years, either. It was intermission during Sing, and he had already driven to Rosie's house, run upstairs, and gotten her flowered dress out of her closet.

The whole time, she hadn't noticed him — or at least she pretended not to. He walked into the dining room. For a moment, he watched her poring over the diner payroll. There was something so strong and dignified about her, he thought — the qualities that always made his heart beat faster when he saw her.

He hated seeing her make the mistake of her life.

Murray thrust his arm forward and let Rosie's dress drop across her books. She looked up with a start.

When Murray spoke, it was in a firm, forceful tone that surprised even himself. "Nathan was wonderful in his show. It's intermission. The seniors start in thirty minutes. You should be there."

Rosie just sat there without saying a word.

"Hannah has fought very hard to create her own life," Murray went on. "What's so wrong with that? Look at you — you're a survivor." He lowered his voice and tried to meet Rosie's downcast eyes. "Rosie, I'm asking you to come with me."

Still no reaction. There was so much Murray wanted to say, so many words that he could never quite put together. But it all boiled down to one thing, one simple feeling he'd held inside for too long.

"I love you, Rosie," he said tenderly. "Put on the dress. . . ."

He held out his hand and waited, but Rosie never did look up.

Murray felt his spirits sink, but he knew he'd done all he could. If Rosie wanted to destroy her relationship with Hannah, the choice was hers.

Dejected, he turned and headed back to the school, alone.

The gymnasium air was charged with electricity as the senior class gathered around Dominic. Fully made up and dressed in a flowing, futuristic costume, he showed no signs of his injuries.

In fact, as much as Hannah hated to admit it, he actually looked handsome.

As Dominic looked from face to face, everyone fell silent. Then, hesitantly, he began to speak.

"I . . . um . . . I never cared for this school . . . and I almost got out of it without knowing what I was missing. I thought, 'Sing? Yeah, sure,' you know? But then — I don't know, somehow. . . ." He shrugged. "Here I am."

Broad smiles broke out all around. Hannah looked at Miss Lombardo, who was beaming.

Hannah didn't know what had happened to Dominic. Whatever had hurt him so much seemed also to have changed him. Now, minutes from the start of Sing, she felt so excited her stomach was fluttering. And she didn't have too much trouble stifling the guilt she felt inside — guilt over feeling *happy* that Dominic had been beaten up.

All heads turned as one of the gym doors flew open. "Go get 'em," Mr. Marowitz called in.

Dominic turned to the seniors. His eyes were on fire. He raised his fist in the air. *"VICTORY-Y-Y-Y!"*

Hannah could barely feel her feet touch the ground as she ran toward the auditorium.

Chapter 23

"Okay, you guys are on after the first scene. Letitia, move to the left so the props people can go through! Denise, spit out the gum. Come on, come on, it's starting!"

Waving her arms, Hannah lined up a group of dancers backstage. Another group was already huddled together onstage, waiting for the curtain to go up.

She looked over her shoulder to see that the audience was in total darkness. A shiver ran through her as she waited for the show to begin.

Suddenly the floorboards shook with an explosion of sound. Fragments of light shot through the auditorium, and one of them picked out Clarissa. Her fingers flew over the synthesizer as a voice boomed over the speakers.

"LONG, LONG AGO, IN THE MIDDLE OF A GREAT EMERALD-GREEN SEA, THERE FLOATED AN ISLAND KINGDOM. AND ON THAT ISLAND THERE LIVED A HIGHLY ADVANCED CIVILIZATION. . . ."

Whaccckk! A drummer suddenly kicked into a rock beat — and the audience went wild!

Hannah felt the blood rush to her head. A huge grin spread across her face. Behind her, the dancers hugged each other one last time.

Her heart pounding, she turned to watch the opening scene.

And that's when she became aware that *she* was being watched — by Dominic.

She turned to face him. As their eyes met, Hannah was startled by the intensity she felt. In a soft voice, Dominic asked, "So . . . what do we do now?"

"Now? Well, umm, take your place for the opening — "

"That's not what I mean."

Hannah blushed. She knew exactly what he meant. "Well . . . am I going to ever see you again?"

"I'm not going anywhere."

Hannah heard the words. They made her happy, but she didn't want them to. How could she forget what Dominic had done? How could she forgive the heartbreak he had caused her and her family?

But she couldn't help herself. *This* Dominic was different — at least it seemed that way. If she could only get some sort of *sign* from him, some indication that this time he was for real. . . .

Her eyes probed deeply into his. And he looked back at her with a fierceness that seemed to boil just below the surface. Only this time,

Hannah could swear it wasn't anger or bitterness behind his eyes.

It looked like love.

Gently, almost imperceptibly, he nodded his head. Hannah smiled. She had her sign.

They stood silently together, watching the opening number come to a close. The audience was going crazy — and this was only a warm-up. She caught a glimpse of Nathan in the balcony, watching the show with wonder. When she started to think of her mother, she forced the image out of her mind. There was no way Hannah was going to let herself get upset right now.

She checked to see that the dancers were ready, then smiled at Dominic. "Break a leg," she whispered.

But Dominic was deep in thought. "You know," he said, "when we win this thing, those underclassmen ain't gonna have any reason to remember Sing . . . and we *are* gonna win."

Hannah nodded tentatively. She wasn't sure what he was getting at.

"Question is," he continued, "do we want to?"

For a long moment she looked at him, trying to understand. Then, slowly, it all began to make sense.

As Dominic took his place on stage, she became lost in a whirlwind of thoughts.

The rumpled, angry man snaked his way through the lobby to the pay phones. The audience's applause felt like a knife in his side. He picked up a receiver, dropped in a quarter, and punched a number.

"Police," said a voice on the other end.

When the man spoke, his voice was a choked snarl. "Yes, this is Elliot Frye, with the New York State Board of Education. I need some men . . . lots of men!"

Naomi stood on the steps of the Palace of Atlantis. She looked out into the audience and pronounced, "When this island explodes, we will surely die!"

Around her, the chorus of citizens mumbled to each other.

Another student, playing a scientist, put out his hand to shush them. "That is why we all must leave here as soon as possible — and never return."

The music began. Hannah tried to swallow a lump in her throat as Dominic stepped forward to address the crowd.

"There is no island nearby that can support all of us. We must leave," he said. He paused, looking every inch the great leader. "But we cannot go together."

One of the girls gestured around to the others onstage. "But we can't . . . we can't leave here . . . we can't leave each other. . . ."

Choked back with tears, she could barely finish her lines. And Hannah knew why — for the first time, the girl realized she was speaking for the entire senior class of Brooklyn Central High.

Dominic took center stage as the music swelled. "We have no idea what other lands may lie beyond the great waters," he said. "We must take our chances on the waves, and scatter like seeds before the wind. We will take the memory of the good times. And for those darkest of times, we will take what we can of the light!"

One of the tenors from the senior chorus stepped forward and began to sing.

He was joined, in perfect harmony, by another senior.

Some of the boys started to leave the stage, preparing for the great Atlantis catastrophe. But they were pulled back by a group of girls.

Then, one girl stepped forward and wailed out, "Celebrate!" And suddenly the mood changed. Clarissa pounded a dance beat on the synthesizer, and the stage exploded with movement.

The first singer stepped forward and sang a line.

Suddenly, he was answered by a group from way in back of the balcony.

The audience screamed their approval as the singer and the choir continued to trade lines of the song across the auditorium.

The balcony singers made their way to the stage, driving the audience around them into an even greater frenzy.

On the stage, the set slowly changed — and by the time the two groups met, they were surrounded by a huge altar with rows and rows of burning candles. The flickering flames reflected off the dancers as they formed a circle and finished their song of hope for the future.

Finally, Mr. Frye said to himself. His eyes lit up as he saw two policemen come through the front door. "Thank heavens you're here!" he said. "I want this thing stopped!"

They gave him a curious look as they rushed by him.

"Officer Pellegrino, did you hear me?" Mr. Frye shouted. "I want this thing stopped!"

"What are you, crazy?" Officer Pellegrino said. "That's my daughter up there!"

He turned back toward the crowd that was overflowing out the auditorium door.

His eyes practically popping out of his head, Mr. Frye screamed, "I WANT THIS THING STOPPED!"

The cops froze. From the back of the auditorium, heads turned. Slowly, Officer Pellegrino walked toward Mr. Frye.

Mr. Frye swallowed hard as he felt himself being picked off the ground.

In a voice barely above a growl, Officer Pellegrino said, "Shut up, small-fry."

Mr. Frye sputtered helplessly as Officer Pellegrino dropped him to the floor and walked back to see the show.

By now the crowd was on its feet. Dominic was leading a group of the senior boys in an incredible dance combination. When the dance ended, the entire class turned to the altar and grabbed a candle. Singing at the top of their lungs, they descended into the audience, their faces glowing in the candlelight.

Hannah watched the procession snake through the aisles, up the stairs, and into the balcony. She looked from face to transfixed face in the audience. In the back, she caught a glimpse of Mr. Marowitz putting his arm around Miss Lombardo.

And then her heart stopped. She blinked her eyes to make sure she wasn't seeing things.

But the dress was unmistakable. The same flowered dress that her mom wore to all the most special occasions. She fought back a tear of joy as Rosie took her seat next to a proud, smiling Murray.

The auditorium rocked with the final chorus. Each senior, from the shyest to the most spectacularly talented, sang full-throated and loud. On the stage, only one group of singers was left. Slowly, they moved forward as the music swelled to a crashing finish.

Long after Clarissa had taken her hands away from the synthesizer, long after all instruments had fallen silent, the voices soared upward.

When they finished, the audience was left in a stunned silence. One by one, the seniors blew out their candles, said good-bye to each other, and began to walk away in different directions. Clarissa began playing a sad, haunting melody.

It was an eerie, ambiguous moment, just the

way they'd planned it. But Hannah realized now that it couldn't end this way. There was something she had to do.

"STOP!" she suddenly burst out as loud as she could. "Hold everything!"

Chapter 24

The music stopped. Hannah walked onto the stage, squinting into the light. A confused buzz swept over the audience.

She stepped in front of the performers and looked out over the crowd. "It's a good show, isn't it? I was watching it from back there and . . . whew! It's really good, you know?"

Now both the audience and the performers were whispering among themselves, wondering what Hannah was up to.

"I mean, the costumes! Look at these outfits!" Hannah walked back to one of the dancers and fingered the fabric of her skirt. "Great, huh? And these sets! And how about that music? Do you believe it?"

Hannah felt petrified. She had no idea what she was going to say next — but underneath it all, she knew exactly what she was doing.

"And, you know," she continued, "if we finished in time, we'd probably win . . . probably."

She took a deep breath. Out of the corner of her eye, she spotted Rosie, looking panicked.

Hannah began to pace the stage. She felt her throat close up with emotion. Keep it together, she said to herself. "But listen . . . we're the *seniors*. We're going to graduate in a few weeks. And maybe we stay in Brooklyn, maybe we go far away. But we know . . . we know right now just how good this can be. We *lived* it, and there's nothing like it. Not here, not anyplace — 'cause we were there. Together." She took a deep breath. "Isn't there something we can leave behind — something we can give the underclassmen so they'll know how we feel?"

Hannah gestured out to the seniors in the aisles. She saw Dominic staring at her. "Don't you see? Doesn't anybody?"

She looked from one face to the other. And out of the confused, embarrassed silence came a firm "Yes."

Hannah spun around. It was Dominic. She stared at him, wild-eyed with gratitude. After all, this was *his* idea.

Behind her, Denise Popolato suddenly called out, "Yeah!"

One by one, all the seniors nodded and agreed with her.

And suddenly from the balcony, Zena spoke up. "Yes!" Hannah's face burst into a smile as the underclassmen joined in. Her message was hitting home.

Finally, from the back of the auditorium, Miss

Lombardo shouted out her agreement. And as Hannah's eyes shot down to her mother, she could see a tearful, silent nod.

Dominic hopped onto the stage. Looking at an imaginary watch on his hand, he called out to the audience in mock disappointment, "Oh, no! Looks like we're overtime! Ain't no way *we're* going to win now. And if it ain't us. . . ."

In the balcony, the juniors and sophomores began to mutter to each other in confusion. Dominic threw his head back and yelled up to them, "DO YOU WANT IT?"

"YEEEAAAAHHH!" the underclassmen roared.

Hannah looked up to see Zena springing from her seat. "We won?" She turned to Nathan, who was sitting next to her. "Did we win?"

Nathan looked as if he would burst with happiness. "We won! We won!"

Zena threw her arms around him. The entire junior and sophomore class rose up, screaming and hugging one another.

Hannah laughed as she heard Cecelia's voice ring out, "I knew it! I won!"

The audience began to stand in waves. Rosie led the applause, her face glistening with tears.

In the back of the audience, Mr. Marowitz pulled Miss Lombardo into an ecstatic embrace.

Right below Hannah, the judges looked at one another, shrugged, and threw their score pads aside.

Hannah had never felt happier in her life. The spirit of Sing was going to carry on after graduation, no matter what happened to Central.

And when she turned to Dominic, she could swear she saw moisture in his eyes. He raised his eyebrows and smiled, as if to say, "So? How did I do?"

Hannah answered the unspoken question by throwing her arms around him, as a spontaneous chorus of voices began to sing. It was a song of togetherness and unity, a song that promised these students — this community — would never say good-bye.

One by one, the entire audience joined in — except for Dominic and Hannah. But as their lips met, they were singing the promise, too.

To each other.